Fear for Your Life

C. M. Sutter

AUTHOR'S NOTE

This book is a work of fiction by C. M. Sutter. Names, characters, places, and incidents are products of the author's imagination or are used solely for entertainment. Any resemblance to actual events or persons, living or dead, is entirely coincidental.

The scanning, uploading, and distribution of this book via the internet or any other means without the permission of the publisher is illegal and punishable by law. Please purchase only authorized electronic editions, and do not participate in or encourage electronic piracy of copyrighted materials. Your support of the author's rights is appreciated.

About the Author

C. M. Sutter is a crime fiction author who resides in Tampa, Florida.

With more than thirty books published in the thriller and crime fiction genres, she can often be found with a laptop in hand and writing at every opportunity.

She is an art enthusiast and loves to create gourd birdhouses, pebble art, and handmade soaps. Gardening, bicycling, fishing, playing with her dog, and traveling the world are a few of her favorite pastimes.

C. M. Sutter
http://cmsutter.com/
Contact C. M. Sutter
Sign up for C. M. Sutter's newsletter

Fear for Your Life
Detective Mitch Cannon-Savannah Heat Thriller
Series, Book 5

A lone high heel found on a sidewalk and a ticketed car set the week in motion for Savannah Homicide Detective Mitch Cannon, and each day gets worse. Bodies are discovered with only one thing in common—a lack of internal organs.

Is somebody in the Hostess City of the South conducting satanic rituals with innocent people or, even worse, trafficking organs to the highest bidder?

When all other leads fail, the chance sighting of a vehicle in question gives Mitch and his partner, Devon Rue, the break they're looking for. Yet what they discover turns the case completely upside down.

See all of C. M. Sutter's books at:
http://cmsutter.com/available-books/

Find C. M. Sutter on Facebook at: https://www.facebook.com/cmsutterauthor/
Don't want to miss C. M. Sutter's next release? Sign up for the VIP e-mail list at:
http://cmsutter.com/newsletter/

Chapter 1

The moonless night was exactly what Teddy and Chase were looking for. The streets had gone quiet since the bars closed, with most tourists finding their way back to their hotel rooms. Young locals had a different plan. They knew where the after-bar parties were and had no intentions of calling it a night until the early morning hours. After all, the weekend had started, and the ladies were out in droves.

The two men weren't searching for the next party. They were on the hunt, and any woman on foot was fair game. A female was easier to manage than a guy, and that night, the women would be ripe for the picking.

Teddy drove while his brother, Chase, looked up and down every street in the historic district, where most of the bars and restaurants were located. Chase was larger and stronger, the perfect person to do the grabbing. He watched for movement. That night could be the one. Ever since Chase, the eldest of the two, had driven his van from Macon to Savannah several days earlier, they'd done their best to score but hadn't had any luck. Tonight would be different. Teddy felt it in his bones and didn't want to disappoint his brother.

"You sure we can do this?" Teddy asked.

"Yep. It's not a big deal. Grandpa taught us how to hunt, remember? I've done my research, and this could make all the difference in the world." Chase gave Teddy a grin. "I already have my best contacts set up. It's a no-brainer."

Teddy's eyes darted to the illuminated clock on the dash—2:21 a.m. There had to be a woman somewhere walking the street, even if she was just going to her parked car. The bars had closed nearly a half hour earlier, and the party crowd was leaving the area.

"There!" Chase leaned forward and pointed out the windshield. He got a better look then nodded as if satisfied. "That's what I'm talking about! Damn, it's about time."

Teddy laughed. "Dude, we've only been driving around for fifteen minutes. Climb in the back and get ready to pull open the side door. I'll slow alongside her and ask directions. When she comes closer, you jump out and snatch her up."

Chase rubbed his hands together. "I'm more than ready." He stepped over the console to the back of the van, which was already prepared for their guest. Duct tape, zip ties, a rag to gag her with, a flashlight, and rope sat in a cardboard box. A medium-sized cooler sat next to the box and had plenty of ice and celebratory drinks inside. An open sleeping bag with a tarp spread over it lay in the rear space, which was devoid of back seats. The van was a personal hell on wheels for the unlucky woman who would be scooped up and dragged inside.

They didn't want to know her name or hear her pleas. That would make her a real person and not just an object of their obsession. The plan was to immediately gag her and cover her mouth with duct tape then tie her to the large eye bolts screwed into the van's inner walls. She would be at their mercy, and they could have all night and tomorrow with her. The purpose was twofold, but the kill, when that time came, was paramount.

"Okay, I'm ready to stop. Once she comes to the window, leap out." Teddy lowered the passenger-side window and called out to the girl as he pulled to the curb. From the way she was dressed and the way she walked, it seemed clear that she'd just left one of the bars. Her high heels made her less stable on her feet, and because she was wobbly, her guard and apprehension were down too. Teddy ran his fingers through his long blond hair before talking. "Excuse me. I'm lost. Can you tell me how to get to that historic hotel on East Congress?"

She laughed as she crossed the sidewalk toward him. "They're all historic, dummy."

"What did you say? I can't hear you." Teddy nodded at Chase when she reached the open window.

"I said they're all—"

Chase grabbed the handle, yanked open the door, and grabbed the woman off the sidewalk. He tossed her into the van and slammed the door as Teddy floored the gas pedal. They were gone in under ten seconds.

She screamed and bucked, and with each cry for help, Teddy twisted the volume knob on the radio. Her panicked cries would go unheard. As Chase straddled her, he forced the rag into her mouth, sealed it with duct tape, then zip tied her to the ropes that were already strung through the eye bolts. The nameless woman was doomed, and the expression on her face told her assailant that she knew it.

Chase slapped his hands together as Teddy pointed the nose of the van toward his house on the edge of town. "There. She's contained for now. Let's go home and celebrate our first joint success."

"Yep, we have twenty-four hours before we need to do what we need to do. Let's have some fun, drink, and relax. Tomorrow night, we'll dump her out near Skidaway Island."

"Sounds good to me." Chase cracked open two beer bottles and passed one to Teddy.

Teddy clinked bottles with his brother. "It's remote and densely wooded, and there's plenty of marshland in the area. Nothing other than wildlife, and she won't be discovered for weeks if she's found at all. After I pull off the main road and into the woods, nobody will ever know we were there."

Chase chuckled. "Sounds like the perfect dumping grounds to me."

Chapter 2

It was early afternoon on Saturday, a day we'd been looking forward to as a family. My partner, Devon, and I made sure we had the day off—murder cases or not. It was Meg's fortieth birthday, a milestone, and we weren't about to let her forget it. Mom, my sister, Marie, and I had been planning the event for weeks, and after getting a promise from my brother-in-law, Jeff, not to slip up, we asked him to invite his and Meg's friends to our family home for the party. The cousins would play with each other and Gus, the adults would cook and drink, and everyone would enjoy the afternoon well into the night. Designated drivers and babysitters were attending to help if needed.

The weather couldn't have been more perfect as we set up the party space that went from the kitchen out to the deck and flowed down to the backyard. Wispy clouds and a bright-blue sky promised a day of uninterrupted outdoor entertainment. Streamers, black balloons, and signs reminding Meg of her age were taped to every door and tacked to every tree. She would get the business from us because that was the kind of family we were. Everyone got roasted on their special day. It was a rite of passage in the Cannon family, and Meg would happily suck it up and take her turn.

At three o'clock, I received the text I'd been anticipating from Jeff. He said they were en route and would reach the house in fifteen minutes. All the guests had parked on the next block then walked to the house to hide until Jeff, Meg, and the kids came in. It would be the typical surprise birthday party but one everybody enjoyed.

In a quick return text, I reminded Jeff that they needed to come in through the front door. As far as Meg knew, we were having a simple family birthday party with burgers and hot dogs on the grill, gifts, cake, and ice cream. Deep down, I was sure she knew better.

The guests headed into the den to wait while Marie, Mom, Rue, and I watched out the window. When Jeff's SUV rounded the corner, I yelled out that as soon as they walked in, the entire group needed to jump out and wish Meg a happy birthday.

"Here we go, everyone! They're coming up the sidewalk. Let them get in the door before you jump out."

Whispers and chuckles sounded until I shushed everyone, then it was dead silent. As usual, Meg just walked in, then she nearly hit the ceiling when twenty-five people poured out of the den and yelled "Happy Birthday!"

She turned ten shades of red, punched Jeff, then punched me and Marie. She wagged her finger at Mom while we all got a good laugh at her expense.

"What the hell! You guys got me good."

"And the party is just beginning," I reminded her.

Meg groaned. "Just wait, brother. Your fortieth is the last one, and you'll pay dearly."

We all headed to the backyard, and by the look on her face, Meg was truly surprised. "Wow! This is awesome. You guys went above and beyond what was necessary."

"No way," Marie said. "I remember my fortieth, and nobody had mercy on me. It's your turn."

Meg laughed. "That's what I'm afraid of."

I grinned at the kids, who were already running around the yard, chasing and being chased by Gus. They squealed in delight, and the look on Mom's face was priceless. Birthdays and holidays made family time so important.

Rue and I headed to the grill with the platters of dogs and burgers while Jeff and Meg mingled with guests. Marie and Mom set out the appetizers, condiments, and beverages. The tables and chairs had been set up earlier.

Rue watched the grill while I went inside and started the playlist of Meg's favorite classic rock tunes. She blew me an air-kiss when I stepped back outside.

So far, the day was going perfectly, and after the meal, the roasting would begin. That was the part I looked forward to the most.

My phone vibrated in my pocket, meaning a text had come in, so I slipped away to a shady spot to view the screen. I imagined it had to be from someone at the precinct, yet they all knew we were celebrating Meg's birthday. I tapped the message, and it was from our boss, Royce. It was a heads-up that might need our attention tomorrow or Monday when our workweek began. He said a lone high heel was found on the sidewalk only a block from the bar district, and a ticketed car had sat at the curb overnight a hundred feet farther down the street. I grimaced and scanned the yard, and since nobody was watching me, I made a quick call.

"Hey, Boss," I said when Royce picked up. "What do you know about the ticketed vehicle?"

"It's a 2012 blue Honda Civic that belongs to a twenty-three-year-old single female named Valerie Dawson. SVU tracked down her family, and they gave them a few names to call."

"Friends of hers?"

"Yep. So far, she's considered unaccounted for. If she doesn't pop up by the end of the day, especially because of that high heel lying on the sidewalk, her parents are going to fill out a missing person report."

"Did they identify that shoe?"

"The parents didn't, but one friend, Sherry Lyman, who she was out with last night, said Valerie was wearing black heels."

"So I assume the high heel was black?"

"That's correct. For now, it's out of our hands, but I wanted you to be aware. I'm sure SVU will be looking for cameras in the area and at the last bar the girls were at."

"Which was?"

"Sparky's, and they closed at two a.m."

"Got it."

"So, how's the party going?"

"Couldn't be better. Meg is in for the roasting of her life after we eat."

Royce chuckled. "As she should be. Have a great time and tell her happy birthday for me."

"Will do." I hung up and rejoined Devon at the grill. It looked like the first round of burgers and dogs were about done.

"Where'd you disappear to?" Rue asked.

"Curiosity got the best of me. A text came in from Royce alerting me to a possible missing twenty-three-year-old woman."

Devon frowned. "Why us? Doesn't sound like our department."

I shook my head. "I know. Just a heads-up on his part. Evidently, a lone high heel was found about a hundred feet from her overnight and ticketed parked car."

"Shit."

I swatted the air. "It isn't our case, and today is all about Meg. I probably shouldn't have called Royce, and if anyone other than you knew I did, I'd be in big trouble."

"Nobody is going to hear it come from my mouth. Anyway, the first burgers and dogs are hot off the grill."

"Good, and I'll let the ladies decide who goes first."

We spent the next hour eating and enjoying everyone's company. Birthday cake, coffee, and juice for the kids came after that. The roasting, some containing colorful stories and memories, would take place over drinks later. During that time, the kids would be in the house watching movies and playing video games with the sitter.

The meal, the opening of gifts, and even the off-color jokes aimed at Meg would make it a birthday she wouldn't soon forget.

Everyone had a great time, and the crowd began to thin around ten o'clock. While the cousins dozed on the couch, the remaining grown-ups relaxed, reminisced, and enjoyed a few bottles of wine. We called it a night at eleven thirty, a respectable hour, and Meg's babysitter drove the family home.

I said good night to Rue, told him I would talk to him the next day, and made sure he was fine to drive. The trip from my house to his own was under seven minutes.

Mom and I cleaned up while Marie got the kids in their jammies and off to bed.

"What a great party that was." Marie, who had just come downstairs, sighed then pitched in with the cleanup.

I laughed. "And Meg took all that razzing like a trouper."

"I raised strong kids," Mom said. "You three can take anything."

"Like you can't? You're the toughest seventy-year-old I know."

Mom grinned at me. "Thanks, honey, but you kind of force it out of us."

Marie patted Mom on the back. "Good one, Mom. Guess Meg isn't the only one who deserves to be razzed."

Chapter 3

The next morning, I woke to my ringing phone. Through blurry eyes, I saw that it was barely eight o'clock. The thought of sleeping in on Sunday and having a leisurely breakfast of pancakes, bacon, and bottomless cups of coffee was upended as soon as I answered my phone. It was Royce.

"You up?"

I tried to speak, but my froggy throat prevented it, so I coughed into my fist and tried again. I had either laughed or talked too much during Meg's party, but regardless, I was hoarse. "I wasn't up, but I am now."

"Sorry, Cannon, but that missing girl was found."

"That's good news. So why the phone call?"

"She's dead. Tapper said he saw several stab wounds around her neck and what looked like defensive wounds on her hands. There could be more. She was partially dressed, and he said there was a lot of blood. After washing her down, he should be able to visually determine how she died unless it's a tox issue."

"Shit." I was wide awake and sat up in bed. "She was found pretty quickly. Where was the body located?"

"Would you believe a fisherman found her this morning along a branch of the Odingsell River? He walked his normal path back to the water's edge and saw one of her legs showing through the marsh grasses."

"Damn. There's a good chance she would have never been found if she was a few feet farther in. The animals and nature can make short work out of a human body left to the elements. What do you need, Boss?"

"All of the detectives at the precinct. There are homes about a mile from where her body was located, and considering the fact that the crime is so new, we need to get ahead of it. We have no idea what kind of person we're dealing with."

"Roger that. I'll need at least a half hour. You know I'm not quite as fast as I was two months ago." I hung up and visualized my relaxing breakfast, and day, going down the drain. I opened my bedroom door and at least caught the aroma of coffee. Somebody was up, and a much-needed cup of joe would get me started. With my bathrobe slipped on, I hobbled down the stairs. My recently broken leg was usually stiff in the morning when I got out of bed.

Mom and Marie sat at the table, laughing about yesterday's events.

Marie glanced up when I entered the kitchen. "Got any breakfast requests, bro?"

"Sure do, but I'll have to pass. I just got a call from Royce, and I'm needed at the precinct."

"That can't mean anything good," Mom said.

"Nope, it sure doesn't. The only thing I have time for is possibly a bowl of instant oatmeal and the cup of coffee I'm taking upstairs with me."

"I'll make you a travel mug to go when you're ready, and the oatmeal will only take a minute."

"Thanks, sis." I poured a cup and headed to my bedroom. After gulping down my coffee, I showered and dressed. By twenty after eight, I was downstairs, where I drank another cup while Marie prepared the oatmeal. I thanked her, shoveled it down, and grabbed the travel mug.

"We'll talk more about the party tonight. I'm sure I'll be ready for some humor by then." I said goodbye and walked outside to my rental. My new Caffeine Metallic Vette wouldn't show up for another month, which was fine. It would be difficult getting in and out of it for a while anyway. I'd decided on the new color because not only was it sleek and gorgeous, but it also had a classy look. The Amplify Orange was cool but rebellious, outrageous, and a color that taunted every other sports car to a race. I didn't need to show off for the twentysomething kids with too much testosterone. I climbed into my white Malibu and headed to the station.

Rue's car was already parked when I turned in to our lot, and from a distance, I saw him entering the building. I was sure to find him plugging quarters into the coffee machine when I passed the lunchroom.

Grasping the handrail, I took the stairs to our floor and peeked around the lunchroom's door. With his coffee already in hand, Rue looked to be pondering his choices of breakfast sweets. Doughnuts, Danish, and granola bars filled the machine next to him. I walked in, pointed at A4, and suggested the Danish.

"If you don't take it, I will. One package of instant oatmeal doesn't go very far."

"Yeah, it does look good, but go ahead. I've got my eyes on that chocolate-glazed doughnut."

"You sure?"

"Yep, so get cracking. I'm hungry."

I pulled a dollar bill out of my wallet and slid it into the slot. The machine sucked it in, I pressed A4, and the Danish dropped to the door at the bottom.

"This should hold me over until lunch. Unfortunately, the pancakes and bacon I visualized for breakfast this morning didn't happen, but that's life. Instant oatmeal and a Danish will have to do."

"So, the victim is that girl you told me about yesterday, right?"

"I think so. I imagine by now, they've identified her unless they haven't found her phone or purse yet. Forensics can use the fingerprint pad in the field if they need to."

Devon nodded. "Unless she isn't in the system."

"Right." I jerked my chin toward the machine. "Buy your doughnut, and let's find out what Royce wants us to do."

With our sugary treats in hand, we continued down the hallway to our boss's office. I gave the partially open door two knocks, and he waved us in.

"Have a seat, guys, so I can bring you up to speed with what I know so far."

We dropped down onto the guest chairs, and Royce began.

He opened the folder lying on his desk. "The 911 call came in at six forty-eight this morning. The fisherman caught a glimpse of her leg in the marsh grass." He looked up at me. "Like I explained to you over the phone."

I gave him a nod and leaned forward.

"Sergeant Riley was contacted, and since the shift change was about to take place, he waited for Mason and Morrow to arrive and sent them to the scene. First responders had already secured the site. There's a handful of officers combing through the grasses and looking for evidence. Riley called Forensics and Tapper, then he called me. As of right now"—Royce tipped his wrist—"everyone is out there except us. I'm staying behind to man the ship."

Devon took his turn. "So should we head out too?"

"Yep, that's the plan. You and the weekend boys can divide up the duties, unless you want to work the city end of things instead."

"As in?" I asked.

"Looking for cameras in the area where the high heel was found. I know none of those businesses are open today, but you can document where all of the cameras are located and pay those places a visit tomorrow. After you do that, you can go into Sparky's and ask the staff about the girl."

I held up my hand. "Do we have a positive ID that the victim is Valerie?"

Royce sighed. "We do. Her parents included photographs of her with the missing person report. The missing persons department forwarded a photo to Riley, who then forwarded one to Tapper. It's been confirmed. The dead woman in the marsh is Valerie Dawson."

"And she was stabbed to death?" I asked.

"Yes, she was stabbed, but regardless of the stab wounds, there may be more to the story. Tapper said she likely died from blood loss. He hasn't ruled out anything else just yet—tox and the like. He'll know more once she's on the table and washed down."

I rubbed my chin. "We could interview that Sherry Lyman friend and find out if anyone else was with them last night."

Royce let out a long puff of air. "Yeah, maybe you two should stay in town. You'll knock out plenty that you'd be doing tomorrow anyway. If Morrow and Mason need more help, I'll call in Bentley and Lawrence."

"What about the parents?"

"They've been notified, but they don't have details since we haven't got anything else to tell them. They did set up a time tomorrow when they'll identify her and talk with Tapper."

"Understood. I think we should interview the friend first. Whatever this friend tells us could lead to more information to investigate."

Royce pushed back from his desk. "Okay, head out. Update me after you talk to Sherry Lyman."

"We need her address, Boss."

"Yep, and I'm texting it to your phone right now."

Chapter 4

Rue and I headed in the general vicinity of my home. Apparently, Sherry still lived with her folks, and they had a house in Thomas Square too. I was curious to see it, and as it turned out, the Lyman home was only two blocks from my own.

It was early for us to be showing up on a Sunday. I assumed Sherry hadn't gone anywhere yet and was possibly still asleep at nine a.m. I parked along the curb, and we walked up the sidewalk of the manicured property. When we reached the porch, Rue rang the doorbell.

I felt bad about stopping in, but murder and death of a friend didn't follow a schedule. We needed to speak with Sherry right away. The only thing she knew at that moment was that Valerie was missing—nothing more.

It took a few minutes before the sound of footsteps got closer then stopped. I imagined whoever was on the other side of the door was sizing us up through the peephole. I held out my badge so there would be no mistaking us for salesmen.

A man who looked to be in his mid-forties, wearing

sleep pants and a T-shirt, answered the door. He ran his fingers through his hair as if to make sure it was lying flat.

"Can I help you officers?"

"Are you Mr. Lyman?" I asked.

He appeared concerned. "I am. Why?"

"And you have a daughter named Sherry?"

"I do." He pointed over his shoulder. "She's in bed asleep. What's this about?"

"Mr. Lyman, may we come in? It's imperative we speak to Sherry. You'll need to wake her up."

"Um, can you tell me why?"

"Sir. You can't help us. Only your daughter can."

He called out over his shoulder. "Mary Beth, go wake up Sherry." He turned back to us. "Please come in."

Rue and I entered the nicely furnished house, and I made the introductions while we stood in the foyer.

"I'm sorry. Where are my manners? Please come into the living room and have a seat," Mr. Lyman said.

Rue and I sat for several minutes before a sleepy-looking young woman with tousled hair came from the hallway area and into the living room. We stood, introduced ourselves, and asked her to have a seat next to her parents. I explained why we were there and said that unfortunately, Valerie had been found dead that morning. I told them that I couldn't go into details about Valerie's death. What we needed to know was every move they had made and everywhere they had gone before parting ways on Friday night.

Sherry began to sob, and we waited for her to compose herself so we could continue the interview. Once she took a gulp of water from the glass that her mom handed her, Sherry began.

"It was Val, Becky, and me together on Friday night.

We each drove separately and met on Congress Street. We went to three bars that night—Delilah's, The Grinch, and Sparky's." She looked from Rue to me then continued. "We closed Sparky's and planned to go on to a house party, but we'd already had enough to drink and decided to call it a night instead." A look of fear took over her face. "Am I going to be arrested for drunk driving?"

I shook my head. "That's not our concern right now, but driving when you've drunk too much could cause problems for you going forward. You could be arrested or cause an accident and have your license revoked."

She glanced at her parents and then at the floor.

"Tell us what took place at each bar, who you spoke with, and if anyone seemed to cause a ruckus at the bar or with you girls."

"Um, I don't recall anything bad happening at any of the bars. We were just having the typical Friday night fun. We do the same thing every Friday night."

"Nobody came on to any of you or seemed to be a pest? Someone who wanted to buy you drinks, or did?"

"Oh yeah. There were two guys at Delilah's who bought beer for us, but we made sure the cans hadn't been opened before the bartender gave them to us."

"Smart thinking, and then?" Rue asked.

"We made small talk with them for a while then moved on to The Grinch. I didn't notice them there."

"And what about at The Grinch and Sparky's? Anything that stood out?"

Sherry looked at me with teary eyes. "No, and I had no idea that would be the last time I'd see Val alive." She leaned into her mother's arms and sobbed. "She was my best friend since junior high. We did everything together."

I nodded. "We're so sorry for your loss. We're almost done here. We'll need Becky's last name and contact information. Also, did those guys at Delilah's give you their names?"

"Yes but no last names. They said they were Scott and Billy, buddies in town for the weekend."

"Did they say from where?"

She shook her head.

"Okay, and how did you ladies part ways when Sparky's closed?"

"They don't have a parking lot, so we all found street parking wherever we could. That's how everyone does it. I guess we each went our own way."

I was well aware of the lack of parking lots in the historic district. A parking lot at any establishment would be a godsend, but few places had that luxury. If they did, the lots would have been small and likely for employees only.

After I glanced at Rue, we stood and thanked the Lyman family for their time, then I handed Sherry my card. "If anything else comes to mind, please call. We'll show ourselves out."

Once seated in the cruiser, I checked the time. It was still too early to pay Sparky's a visit. They didn't open until the lunch hour.

"Let's go to the area where the high heel was found. I know the first responders scoured the sidewalk and curbs for evidence, but I doubt that they were looking for cameras right then. We'll take note of every camera in a two-block area then visit those businesses tomorrow."

"We should also follow Valerie on camera after leaving Sparky's. We'll look at their footage while she was there and then whatever cameras we can find of her walking to her car."

"Absolutely."

I aimed the cruiser north on Abercorn and toward the historic district. Valerie's high heel had been found on the sidewalk at Whitaker Street, two blocks south of Congress. I was familiar with the area, primarily a mix of bars and restaurants, but none were open yet.

The evening hours between six and closing were when the bar and restaurant scene was hopping. After two a.m., when the bars emptied, the streets were all but deserted.

After cutting over on Congress, I turned south on Whitaker, a one-way street. After pulling over at the curb where Valerie's shoe was found, I cut the engine, and we climbed out. Out of habit, I patted my chest pocket to make sure I had my notepad and pen, and I did. We planned to check the buildings for cameras and the ground for clues. To my knowledge, another set of eyes or two had never hurt an investigation.

Over the next hour and in a two-block area, we found six businesses with cameras mounted outside. That didn't necessarily mean they were real cameras or that they'd caught the street, but we would know more after talking to the managers. We still had an hour to go before Sparky's opened for their lunch crowd. The other two bars served only snacks, so they didn't open until after four o'clock.

"Let's walk from Sparky's to Whitaker and note the cameras along that route," I said.

At that time of day, there wasn't a lot of traffic, and curb parking was plentiful. I slid into a spot just outside the front door of the bar, and we headed out on foot.

It was only a two-block walk to the intersection of Congress and Whitaker, but that would still take longer than usual with my stiff leg. I suggested we continue with those additional blocks south on Whitaker until we reached the location where the high heel was found. That time, we would check the opposite side of the street to cover all options. By the time we returned to Sparky's on the opposite side, they'd be open for business.

Rue frowned. "So essentially, Valerie walked nearly four blocks from where she parked her car to Sparky's?"

I shrugged. "If my math is correct, yeah, that's what she did. Seems like quite the distance to find a parking spot."

"Maybe not during the weekend. The bars are crazy busy Friday and Saturday nights."

"I suppose you're right, and it wouldn't seem so far if she wasn't walking alone but—"

Rue finished my thought. "But a somewhat inebriated young woman walking four blocks alone after bar hours could be easy prey."

I let out a groan. "And it looks like she was." We continued down the street, and I pointed at a camera in front of the Bar Association, a popular nightspot with attorneys. I pulled out my notepad and wrote down the name.

"I always thought that place had a catchy name," Rue said.

"Yep, it sure does. I've heard there's a similar nightclub in Charleston called Passing the Bar."

Rue nodded. "We should have a bar specifically for cops."

I grinned and played along while keeping my eyes focused on the buildings. "What would we call it?"

"Behind Bars?" Rue chuckled.

I added my take. "How about Cuffed?"

"Or Savannah Blues?"

"Yeah, I like that one."

We reached the intersection of Congress and Whitaker and headed south on the opposite side of the street from where we had been earlier.

Rue tipped his chin at Margie's, a corner diner with a camera outside that pointed toward the entryway, not the street. He wrote it down anyway.

Once we reached the location where we had been before, we turned back.

Devon gave the area a final look. "That didn't help much."

"No, it didn't, but normally during bar hours, there's plenty of foot traffic and beat cops out and about. Once everything shuts down, the bar crowd heads to the after-parties."

"And unfortunately for Valerie, the cops leave too," Rue said.

Chapter 5

We reached Sparky's at twelve fifteen and walked in. The bar was much darker than the outdoor natural light, and it took a few seconds for our eyes to adjust. Music played but at a much lower volume than it did at night. Two men sat at the bar and three couples at the tables. On weekend nights, people were lucky to find a seat at all.

Rue and I bellied up to the bar. Since we were on duty, we would have to limit our beverages to the nonalcoholic type.

"Hey, T. J. How's it going?" I asked.

With a towel draped over his shoulder, the bartender headed our way then placed two coasters in front of us. "Good as anyone could expect on a Sunday." He tipped his wrist and grinned. "Since it's only fifteen minutes into my shift and I get off at four." He looked from Rue to me. "How's it hanging at Habersham?"

I shrugged. "Same shit different day."

"Yeah, you two don't always work on Sunday. What brings you to the precinct on your day off?"

I groaned. "What do you think? We *are* homicide detectives."

"Yeah, that sucks. So what can I get you?"

"Information," I said.

T. J. looked puzzled. "Information?"

"Yep. Apparently, the young lady who was murdered closed Sparky's on Friday night. That was the last time she was seen alive."

"No shit?"

"No shit. We need to know who was working that night and if they witnessed anyone with the woman in question. We'll need to see the indoor and outdoor camera footage from that night too."

"Yeah, sure. I'll get George."

"T. J.?"

"Yep?"

"Were you working then? Maybe you know the girl."

"No, I had Friday night off. I couldn't even tell you who was scheduled then, but George can. I'll be right back. Wait, let me get you something on the house. A couple of sodas?"

"Thanks. That'd be great," I said.

With two sodas sitting on the coasters in front of us, we waited as T. J. headed to the office to get George, the weekend manager.

Minutes later, a slender middle-aged man with salt-and-pepper hair and glasses headed our way. T. J. returned to the bar, where he refilled the Bloody Marys the customers next to us were drinking.

"What can I help you with, Detectives?" George reached out and shook our hands.

I asked if we could speak to him privately, and he tipped his head toward the office. We gulped down our sodas and followed him.

"Have a seat, guys." He closed the door at our backs. George rounded the desk and sat with his hands folded.

I began. "The body of a twenty-three-year-old woman was found early this morning by a fisherman along the banks of the Odingsell River."

"That's terrible news, but how can I help?"

"She was last seen alive leaving here on Friday night. Saturday morning, she hadn't returned home, and her ticketed car was parked along Whitaker Street. Her folks filled out an official missing person report last night after confirming that she wasn't with any of her friends. Just by pure luck, that fisherman saw her leg through the marsh grass and called 911. She could have been lost forever in the elements like that with the weather and wild animals."

George shook his head. "So because her car was ticketed on Whitaker, you're assuming something happened to her between Sparky's and her car?"

"We know so. We've already interviewed one of the two young ladies she was with Friday night. They closed the bar together and each headed back to their individual cars. That dead girl never made it to her car. In that four blocks between Sparky's and her vehicle, she disappeared. We'll need to speak with every employee who worked that night and see the bar's camera footage from inside and out."

"Sure, whatever you need." George jiggled the computer mouse to his right then began tapping keys. "I'm pulling up the list of staff who worked Friday night until closing and will print it out for you."

"Appreciate it," Rue said. "We'll need their phone numbers too."

George nodded. "I'll add them to the sheet I'm printing."

Seconds later, the printer at his back hummed. The sheet printed, and he placed it on his desk.

George tapped the keys again, I assumed to pull up the entire staff's contact information, then he wrote down phone numbers of the twelve people who'd worked Friday night. He slid the sheet across the desk to me.

"The ones I put the stars next to waited on the customers. The others are cooks or dishwashers and don't have any interaction with them."

"Got it. That's very helpful," I said. "Now, we need to see the footage from midnight to closing. Indoors as well as outside if you have both."

"Yep, give me just a minute to set those parameters."

We waited as George made the adjustments for the day and time.

"You want to start with the indoor cameras?"

"Sure," I said. "How many do you have?"

"Four."

I raised my index finger. "Give me just a second. I need to make a call." I checked my notepad for Sherry's number and called her. "Sherry, it's Detective Cannon. I need to know where you girls were standing or sitting at Sparky's. Were you at a table, the bar, or where? Also, what was Val wearing with those black high heels?"

"She had on black leggings and a wispy long-sleeved top with tiny flowers on it."

"Great, and where were you in the building?"

"We stood at the left side of the bar. There wasn't anywhere to sit, and it's closer to the bathrooms there."

"Okay, thanks." I ended the call and repeated that information to George. "The girls were on the left side of the bar."

"Sure, and that's camera two." With the correct

camera, date, and time set up, George turned the laptop toward us and went about his business.

Within a few minutes, the three girls came into frame. It appeared that they'd just arrived. I checked the time on the footage, 12:17, and Rue wrote that down.

The noise level was high, so we couldn't hear the communication between the girls, but it was obvious that they ordered drinks as soon as they got the attention of the bartender. I paused the footage and asked George who that bartender was. I spun the laptop, and he took a look.

"That's Gary Carson, and the other bartender is Beth Myers. They both worked until closing."

"Behind the bar the entire time?"

"Yes, bartending for the whole shift."

"Thanks." I turned the laptop back and waited for Rue to write down the names of the bartenders, then we continued watching. There was talk between the girls and several other customers but nothing that seemed to irritate anyone—just casual chat as people walked by. I kept my voice lowered as Rue and I discussed what we were watching. "I don't see any guys coming on to them or being a nuisance. Looks like a fun night out and nothing more."

Rue agreed. "They're buying all their own drinks too. Let's speed through some of this and get closer to bar-closing time. That'll show us if they walked out alone or with some guys."

"True, but Sherry never mentioned leaving with any guys."

Rue shrugged. "People forget or lie. Cameras don't."

"Good point." I fast-forwarded the video until it was near bar closing. At that point, I set it back to normal speed. We saw Sherry sitting on a barstool while the other two women continued to stand. I imagined they might have taken turns on that stool since no others were available.

"Looks like it's that time. The lights just went on, and the bartenders are yelling out 'last call,'" Rue said.

I pointed at the screen. "There, the girls are leaving." I noted the time again—1:53 a.m. I tipped my head at George. "Okay, can we see the outdoor camera from one fifty a.m. on?"

"Sure."

I turned the computer toward him so he could make the adjustments, which took only a few seconds.

"Here you go. It's ready whenever you are. Just hit Play."

I did, and the video started. People were exiting the bar, talking on the sidewalk, making plans, and heading off. Nobody in the immediate area seemed to be standing off to the side and watching people as they left. Actually, I didn't see anyone outside until Sparky's doors opened and people flooded out. It took several minutes before the girls showed up on the footage. They stood off to the side, talked for a bit, hugged, and each went their own way. Valerie was the only one of the three who walked east. No guys were with them, and nobody appeared to be following her, only people going in the same direction, likely to their cars.

I groaned out a disappointed sigh. I didn't know what I'd been expecting, but I didn't see anything that would help us from the footage inside and in front of Sparky's.

According to George, neither Gary Carson nor Beth Myers was scheduled to work that day. We would stop at their homes and interview each of them before returning to the precinct to see if they'd overheard anything or were part of a discussion with the girls.

Tomorrow, we planned to check all the camera locations along Valerie's walk to her car. Someone with ill intentions might have popped out of a dark alley or doorway after she turned onto Whitaker. It was unlikely that other Sparky's customers had walked that far back to their vehicles, making her an easy and singular target.

Rue read off Beth's address while I drove. I shook my head as I recalled my thoughts from minutes earlier. "That won't work."

Rue frowned. "What won't work?"

"My thoughts of someone popping out of an alley and snatching up Valerie. An opportunist looking for easy prey."

"Go on."

"Well, where would he have taken her? Would he drag her down the sidewalk to his possible apartment above a store while she kicked and screamed?" I asked.

Rue frowned. "Right. That's highly unlikely. What if it was a team effort? He snatched her and had someone waiting in the wings with a vehicle. It would be a tough task for one person to pull over, grab someone off the sidewalk, and drag them to their car without her biting, kicking, and yelling for help."

"Unless he tased her or knocked her unconscious first."

"That's a possibility too." Rue checked the time. "Maybe Tapper has some initial information for us. Valerie has been on the table for over an hour."

Chapter 6

The interview with Beth Myers lasted a short ten minutes. She said she'd worked the opposite side of the bar from Gary on Friday night and didn't speak to anyone on his side. She was swamped with drink orders and didn't have time for socializing.

We thanked her for her time and moved on to Gary Carson's apartment, which was only five blocks from the precinct.

I gave his door on the second floor two raps, and we waited. A voice from inside the apartment called out. Gary, I assumed, wanted to know who was there. I looked at Rue and shrugged. If Gary wanted all his neighbors to know the cops were at his door, then so be it.

I yelled back that we were detectives from the Habersham precinct and needed to speak with him.

Without a peephole to peer through, he would have to take our word for it. I had my badge in hand for the moment the door creaked open.

I assumed that on a Sunday when Gary didn't have

to work, he might be lounging in sleep pants or something of that nature. Maybe he had to brush his hair. I didn't know, but it wasn't the first time that we'd waited at front doors for some time before the occupant opened it.

The door finally opened, and we saw one eyeball. I held my badge in front of it so Gary could clearly see that we were being honest with him.

"Detectives, huh? Okay, what's up?"

"May we come in?" Rue asked. "We have a few questions for you."

Gary rubbed his eyes. "Yeah, I guess."

I took his disheveled appearance to mean he might have been asleep when I knocked. We thanked him, walked in, and told him we wouldn't be long.

He plopped down on the couch without offering us seats. "So, what is this about?"

Rue took the reins. "We're here to talk to you about Friday night. You were working the bar area at Sparky's, right?"

"Yep, that's correct. Was there a complaint about something?"

"No, not at all. One of the young ladies you served that night came up missing after the bar closed. She was found deceased just this morning."

"Holy shit. That's crazy."

"I'd have to agree," Rue said. "There were three girls who stayed on your side of the bar for the time they were there. Names were Becky, Sherry, and Valerie. You waited on them between midnight and closing. Valerie wore a wispy flowered top, and she had long blondish hair."

He wrinkled his forehead. "Yeah, now I remember. They seemed like nice girls."

"Any conversations in particular you had with them?"

"Me?" Gary chuckled. "I listen to the drink orders, make said drinks, and take their money unless somebody wants to run a tab. There is zero time for conversations." He looked from Rue to me. "I don't know if either of you have ever been to Sparky's, especially on a Friday or Saturday night after ten o'clock, but it's a madhouse."

Devon and I had both been there plenty of times, but after ten on a weekend? Chances were that we hadn't. It wasn't often that I stayed out late and drank the night away since there was a more than seventy percent chance that one or both of us would be working the following day.

I took my turn. "Then did you hear any conversations about after-parties or see someone ask them to one?"

Gary shook his head. "I tune people out unless they're waving their hand to get my attention, and that's just because they want a drink. Sorry, but I didn't hear anything other than loud chatter and the music playing."

Disappointed, I was leaning toward Valerie's abduction being a crime of opportunity, not premeditation. After thanking Gary for his time, we left.

I grunted as I plopped down behind the steering wheel. "Damn it. We've got nothing."

"We've got tomorrow, and that's a lot more than Valerie has."

"Yeah, sorry. When you put it that way, I sound like a real ass. Let's head in, see what Royce says, and plan to hit the ground running as soon as those businesses open in the morning. Chances are, if there's a camera within range of where Valerie's heel was found, then we'll see the abduction take place."

Rue chuckled. "If only things were that easy."

It was just after twelve when we walked up to the second floor of our building. We wanted to grab some vending machine food, drop it off in our office, then have a sit-down with Royce. I couldn't remember the last time we had a positive outcome on the first day of talking to people in a murder case. Usually, the pieces began to fall into place close to a week into the investigation. I doubted that this time would be different since so far, we had zilch.

Devon and I backtracked to Royce's office and found it empty.

"That's weird. I wonder where he went."

"Call his cell. It's probably the easiest way to find him," Rue said.

I fished my phone out of my pocket and tapped Royce's name. He picked up immediately.

"Hey, Boss, we're back."

"Good. Come down to Tapper's office immediately."

"Okay, we're on our way." I hung up and was sure my expression was one of bewilderment.

"What's up?" Devon asked.

"Royce wants us to go down to Tapper's office."

"Why?"

"He didn't say. Let's go see what the urgency is all about."

We walked down the stairs we had just gone up. Our lunch would have to wait. Entering Tapper's office and autopsy room on our basement level was always chilling —literally. The temperature was set at a cool sixty-eight degrees year-round, making the rooms seem much colder than on our own office floor. Most of the bodies lying in cold storage had met their fate in a violent manner, murder, and they remained there sometimes for weeks because of the investigations. The bodies of people who'd died of natural causes or car accidents were taken to a hospital's morgue, not one in a police station.

When we walked in, I called out to Royce. He answered from the autopsy room. It didn't take a rocket scientist to know that we were about to view Valerie's body on the table.

I cupped my hand and whispered to Rue as we headed that way. "This is the part I can do without."

He grimaced just as we walked in, and Royce and Tapper stood in front of Valerie's sheet-covered body.

"What's up?" I asked as we approached.

Royce groaned. "First, it appears that Valerie has only been dead for about nine hours."

"But she's been missing since two a.m. yesterday morning," I said.

"That's true," Royce said, "but Tapper has checked her stage of rigor and took her body temperature. Of course, that might be skewed because of—"

"Of what?" Rue asked.

"I'll let Tapper explain."

We turned our attention to our county medical examiner and waited for him to begin.

Tapper sighed. "While at the scene, I wondered why there was so much blood around her torso area. Of course, she was partially dressed, and what was immediately visible were the cuts to her arms and neck region. I assumed she had more stab wounds to her abdomen but wanted her on the table and cleaned up before I verbalized my thoughts."

I frowned. "So she didn't?"

"When I first saw her, I assumed she had been redressed. Her clothes were on her haphazardly, not the way a woman would dress herself. When I removed her clothing back here in the autopsy room, I was stunned by what I saw in front of me." Tapper shook his head. "Her chest cavity was damn near empty—a handful of her organs had been removed. That in itself would throw off her body temperature."

I was sure my bulging eyes gave away my shock. "Did you say her organs were removed?"

"Most of the organs that can be transplanted."

"Excuse my stupidity, but what are they? The ones that were gone?" Rue asked.

"Her heart, liver, kidneys, and lungs are missing from her body. Whoever did this left the pancreas and intestines behind."

"Why would they do that?"

"I can only speculate," Tapper said. "The pancreas sits above the large intestine. I'm guessing the person or people who gutted her, so to speak, didn't want to involve themselves with the intestines."

"So was it some kind of voodoo ritual, or did they do it for profit?" I asked.

Tapper shrugged. "No clue, but in all my years as a medical examiner—"

I cut in. "I doubt that any of us have ever come across this before."

"Another thing that stood out was the fact that the organs were removed meticulously with a sharp knife. The remaining tissue had clean edges." He muttered under his breath. "It wasn't the cut-open-and-yank-out method like when an animal is hunted, killed, and field dressed."

Royce groaned as he looked at us. "Find out if Vice has any CIs who know of people involved in spiritual things, human sacrifice, eating human organs, witchcraft, and so on. This is Savannah for God's sake, and there's a lot of ghostly weird shit that goes on in this city behind closed doors."

"I've never heard of *that* kind of stuff here," Rue said. "It's all just ghost sightings, haunted houses, and cemeteries for the benefit of tourism."

"Check anyway and see what pops. If nothing is discovered, then we'll have to move on to the other motivation."

"Profiting off of human organs?" I asked.

Royce let out an irritated-sounding huff. "Unfortunately, yes, and if that theory holds true and sales are made across state lines, it's considered trafficking human organs, and the FBI would get involved. Organ donation is one thing, but killing someone to harvest their organs is completely unknown territory in our neck of the woods. Chances are the FBI would take over the entire case."

"The entire case? Valerie is the only victim that we know of," Rue said.

"Don't be foolish enough to believe this is an isolated incident, Devon. Whoever is doing this, if that's what it is, probably has a network of buyers. The killers could be traveling from state to state to keep from being discovered."

I added my two cents. "And I'm sure they thought by tossing Valerie out in the marsh like that, she would never be found."

"True, but first things first. Let's try the voodoo angle before going off half-cocked and alerting the FBI. We don't need egg on our faces. Cover all angles and find out everything you can before we make that leap." Royce checked the time. "I'm heading out to the scene. As of right now, Sergeant Riley and his detectives have no idea what Tapper discovered. The weekend shift is his, and we aren't going to step on toes, but the way it seems now is that everyone needs to pitch in on this, weekend or not."

"So should we let Riley decide who does what or…?"

"Go talk to Vice. We may have to work together between all departments since we don't have anyone who specifically deals in this type of thing, but start there. Vice handles all that wackadoodle stuff. See what they know and who they can point you to for an interview."

"Roger that."

Rue and I headed to Vice's wing of the building. It wasn't much of a stretch to get their take on the situation since they did handle local human trafficking, but it was unlikely that they'd ever dealt with a human-organ-trafficking situation.

We entered their department and asked for Sergeant Cal Taylor. He was the commanding officer during the weekend day shift hours. We needed a private sit-down with him before he called in his detectives for their opinions.

The receptionist, Terry, called Taylor's office. She said he would be out in just a minute. Rue and I took seats and watched for his office door to open. When it did, he walked out, and we stood and shook his hand.

"What can I do for you, Detectives?"

"Can we talk privately?" I asked.

"Of course. Let's go into my office."

Once seated, I explained what we knew so far in the disappearance of Valerie Dawson. I told him she'd disappeared Friday night and that her remains were discovered early that morning by a fisherman at the Odingsell River. "What we just learned from Tapper is that most of Ms. Dawson's organs were removed, hopefully postmortem."

Taylor leaned forward. "What the hell?"

I continued. "What we need from your department is knowledge of any occurrences where people removed organs for voodoo stuff, like consuming them or if they were used in spiritual or ritualistic gatherings."

"Wow. There have been situations like that but never with human organs. I mean, that would be considered murder, and our department wouldn't be involved."

"True, but is it so much of a leap to go from sacrificing animal organs to human organs, especially if the people involved were high on toad venom or some other hallucinogen?"

"I see your point, Mitch. Let's get Bobby and Luke in here to see what they think." Sergeant Taylor made a call, talked for a few seconds, then hung up. "They'll be right in. Give any thought to this being organ trafficking?"

"Sure, but Sergeant Royce wants to eliminate it being local voodoo involvement before we alert the FBI."

Taylor nodded. "And that makes perfect sense."

Chapter 7

A knock sounded on Sergeant Taylor's door only a minute later. He called out for them to come in. Detectives Bobby Freeman and Luke St. James walked in and appeared surprised to see Rue and me.

"Grab a couple of chairs, guys. Detectives Cannon and Rue need your opinion on a case they're working."

"Sure thing. Good to see you two. It's been a month or so, right?" Bobby asked as he and Luke opened two folding chairs and sat down.

"Yep, and it seems that we're all too busy to cross paths even though we're in the same building," Devon said.

Luke looked at Taylor. "So, why are we here?"

Taylor jerked his chin my way. "Go ahead, Mitch, and tell them what you told me."

I repeated what Rue and I had just discussed with Sergeant Taylor. "We need help, guys. Have you ever dealt with people who do weird shit like that, possibly contacts who may know those kind of people?"

"Like CIs?"

"Yeah, that's what we were thinking," Devon said. "As Royce put it, he doesn't want us to go off half-cocked and involve the FBI unless we're relatively sure this is an organ-trafficking situation."

"Yeah, I see where you're coming from. You can't backpedal from that," Bobby said.

Taylor took his turn. "In the seventeen years I've been the sergeant in this department, I can't recall a situation like this. How about you guys? Maybe my old age is causing me to be forgetful."

Bobby swatted the air. "You've got a memory like a steel trap, Boss, and you're only fifty-two. Honestly, we've dealt with animal ritual stuff, and those people were arrested for animal cruelty and abuse. They were fined, but human organ cases? Never since I've been on the force."

"So, maybe we can start with those people who have participated in animal sacrifices. They may know someone who is a little more off the rails than they are."

"Yeah, maybe," Luke said as he looked at Taylor. "Want us to pull those files?"

The sergeant nodded. "Go ahead. Whatever we can do to help Homicide."

Rue and I stood, thanked them, then walked to the door. "Appreciate it, guys. Just call my office when you have the files, and I'll come down and pick them up."

"Hope that'll help, Mitch."

Rue and I headed upstairs. Royce had already gone to the scene where Valerie was found, so I would update him over the phone. If he wanted us to remain at the precinct until the detectives returned, we could spend that time reviewing police jackets of the people arrested for animal cruelty and abuse of a corpse. I decided to give him a quick call and find out. I was sure it wouldn't take long for Vice to compile those police files for us.

Back in our office and eating the food that still lay on my desk, I called Royce and told him that Vice only had files on people who'd abused animals. I added that we would be happy to review those files until the detectives and Riley returned to the precinct. He told us to go ahead and said he'd let Riley know. Mason and Morrow would likely be heading back soon since they hadn't found any evidence at the scene and the nearest neighbors were a mile away.

A half hour later, my desk phone rang. It was Bobby letting me know they had nine police jackets of people who had been arrested for animal cruelty in the past. I told him I would be right down to pick them up. I hung up and pushed back my chair. After a good stretch, I stood up.

"I'll be right back. That was Bobby saying the police jackets are ready."

"Good," Rue said. "Reviewing them gives us a legitimate reason to be here on a Sunday afternoon."

With a slap to the doorframe, I walked out but returned with the folders in less than ten minutes.

"Guess we can dig in," Rue said. "I took the liberty of grabbing each of us a cup of coffee while you were gone."

"Thanks, partner. That's exactly what I need." I settled in at my desk, took five of the folders, and gave Rue the other four. I chuckled when he caught sight of one that looked to be a half inch thick. "That's why I gave you less."

"Damn, this person must have kept Vice busy."

Over the next two hours, we read each file, discussed the charges, checked to see if any names of criminals crossed over as known associates, then picked out the four worst offenders. We assumed the less-violent ones were actually trying to fit in with the others and could very well have been at the same sacrificial rituals.

Morrow and Mason had returned to the station an hour earlier, so they sat down with us and listened to us recount what Tapper had said. They were going to look into organ trafficking to see if anything like that had happened lately and where.

It wasn't long before Royce and Riley were back. As a team, we gathered in the conference room and reviewed what we had and what our next move would be.

Royce addressed me. "First thing tomorrow, I want you and Devon to check camera footage on Whitaker Street. If you're lucky, you might actually catch the abduction."

I had to be honest with Royce so he wouldn't get his hopes up too high. "We didn't see cameras outside any stores in that exact spot. Actually, the closest camera to where Valerie's heel was found was a block away."

He raised his hands. "Whatever. See what you can find. We need to eliminate what the cameras did or didn't catch before we can move on to anything else."

"Yes, sir."

Riley took his turn. "Tomorrow starts a new work-week. How are we going to handle this? Everyone on OT or see what happens?"

Royce rubbed his chin. "By the end of our shift tomorrow, we'll have a better idea of where we stand. Either the cameras will catch something, or my crew will learn more from these idiots with the police jackets. No matter what, I'll update you."

"Sounds good. Why don't you three get out of here

and enjoy what's left of your Sunday? I hear there's a few baseball games on TV later. You've put in more than enough time for today. We'll finish up and I'll touch base with the night crew."

Royce slapped his hands together then nodded at Rue and me. "You heard the sergeant. Let's get the hell out of here."

I was happy to go home and have supper with my family instead of heating up leftovers in the microwave. It was a beautiful June day, almost evening, and a beer on the deck was calling my name. I would have loved to invite Devon over for a couple of cold ones and supper, but I knew our conversation would turn to shop talk, and once in a while I wanted to enjoy time at home without the precinct being mentioned. I was sure my family would appreciate it.

Devon and I parted ways at our vehicles, and I climbed into my rented Malibu.

Rue gestured for me to roll down my window. "When is that Vette showing up?"

"Not soon enough, and it's pure torture to wait every day."

He laughed and waved me off.

I couldn't wipe the grin off my face every time I thought about turning over the engine and hearing that low growl. One of these days, and as soon as the car was broken in, I planned to take Rue out for the ride of his life. We would hit some back road that went on forever and didn't have a single stop sign or crossroad to worry about.

Chapter 8

All of the organs had been put on ice and were delivered that morning—all except the kidneys. The heart, lungs, and liver had a short shelf life and needed to be moved quickly. If they weren't viable when the buyer got them, Chase would lose the money and the customer. Those organs fetched an outrageous price, but most of that money went to the second and third buyer. The kidneys were tough and lasted for up to thirty-six hours on ice. Each kidney would fetch a great price for the brothers. Chase had been making phone calls after they'd killed that woman, and he finally decided on Mr. Harris, a buyer who would give him the price he needed. The man explained that as the middleman and the person with the most risk, he also needed to make a good profit when selling to the final buyer, who, through his contacts, would deliver the kidneys to the hospital for transplant.

They settled on fifty thousand dollars apiece—or a steal at ninety-five thousand for both kidneys. Mr. Harris agreed, and Chase was ecstatic. The delivery was set for ten o'clock that night in Augusta.

"See, bro, we do this a few times and then live the life for a couple of years. We won't have to kill another person during that time. We'll spend the money wisely, buy a few toys, and lie around until noon every day."

"What about Macon?" Teddy asked.

"What about it? I only moved there because of Tracy, and she and I are ancient history. There's nobody there I give a shit about anymore. No girlfriend, no family. Mom and Dad are too busy living the life in Bluffton, and neither of us see them anyway. They're too busy acting like hot shit and boating every weekend with their Hilton Head friends. If you recall, they wrote us off a long time ago."

"Yeah, I know. So what are you saying? Are you moving back to Savannah?"

Chase grinned. "Why not? Like I said, we'll harvest a few more organs, sell them, and then sit back for a while. We can do our own boating up and down the Savannah River, sipping cocktails just like the big shots do."

"That sure sounds nice."

"It's a reality, bro. All we have to do is play it safe and then get rid of each body out in no man's land. There's plenty of places like that in low country between here and Charleston."

Teddy grinned. "I'll drink to that." He clinked beer bottles with his brother and resumed watching the base-ball game on TV.

Chapter 9

To everyone's surprise, I was home at a reasonable time.

"I can't believe what I'm seeing," Marie joked. "Since when on a Sunday when you're called in to work are you back by suppertime? We can actually eat together as a family."

I chuckled. "Since there's nothing we can do until business hours tomorrow. We have to look at camera footage in the bar district and see if we get lucky, but enough shop talk."

Mom agreed with a "hallelujah."

"So, what's for supper?" I asked.

"Swedish meatballs over noodles and a side of green beans," Mom said.

"That sounds great. How soon before we eat?"

Marie looked at the clock. "Twenty minutes or so."

"Okay, I'm going to shower and change clothes."

That cold beer I was going to have before supper would be enjoyed later under the full moon. I looked forward to it, and Mom and Marie were welcome to join me.

After eating that delicious meal and listening to the girls tell me how they'd spent the day, Marie and I cleaned up the kitchen. Della and Chloe had fifteen minutes left of the movie they'd been watching before supper and then it was off to bed. Once they were tucked in, I grabbed three beers out of the fridge, got Marie and Mom's attention, and nodded toward the patio door.

"Gonna join me? The full moon will be right above us, and I can't think of anything better to look at while enjoying a beer."

Mom grinned. "That reminds me of the night on the ship's balcony when we did the very same thing."

I laughed. "And then everything went to hell the next day."

Mom held up her hands. "We had some fun, didn't we? The trip wasn't a complete loss."

I hugged her. "That was a birthday vacation for the books, but I don't want to repeat it."

"Good. Next year, it's an RV vacation, and we're staying on dry land. Maybe a trip to the Smoky Mountains."

Marie nodded. "That sounds nice and relaxing."

I had to say it even in jest. "I hear there are a lot of bears in that area."

Marie punched me in the shoulder. "You suck."

I laughed, opened the slider, and waved at them to come outside with me. It was a crystal-clear night with little humidity, and the moon was full and bright. I would never get tired of that sight or spending quality time with my family. I twisted off the beer caps and passed the bottles out. We spent nearly an hour outside enjoying each other's company. Mom always liked to reminisce about us as children, and they were usually good stories.

By ten o'clock, we'd gone inside, the house was quiet, and everyone else was asleep. As I lay in the comfort of my bed and the safety of my home, I wondered what Valerie's last moments had been like and what had happened during the full day she'd spent alive with her captor. It was something I would never know, yet those kinds of questions always haunted me. I closed my eyes and drifted off.

I woke Monday morning refreshed and thankful that I'd gotten a full night's sleep. That seemed to happen less and less as June turned into July and July into August. Criminals always seemed to be more active in the summer months, maybe because there were more tourists to take advantage of or maybe because the hot, sticky days took their toll. No matter the reason, our homicide department was always the busiest in the summer.

My phone hadn't rung yet, so I hoped to be able to enjoy a sit-down breakfast instead of a piece of toast jammed into my mouth as I bolted out the door. Since I was still recuperating from my broken leg and arm, bolting out the door was impossible anyway. I walked okay but at a slower pace.

As I sat at the table with my mom, my sister, and my nieces, I hoped for a productive day. So far, I felt lucky. I was able to eat an uninterrupted breakfast of scrambled eggs, sausage links, hash browns, and toast. I filled my travel mug with coffee, wished everyone a good day, and headed to the precinct.

Rue had arrived before me, and as I entered our office, he passed on a message from Royce. Our briefing would start at eight o'clock—ten minutes away. He'd said there was a lot to discuss and he wanted to get an early start.

I pulled the lid off my mug, peered inside, and saw only a swallow of coffee left.

"Need a coffee?" I asked before I even sat down. "My mug is pretty much empty, and if it's going to be a long meeting—"

"Yeah, let's go."

We headed down the hallway, and Rue mentioned that he thought Royce and Bleu were going to announce overtime at the briefing.

"I wouldn't doubt it. They need to catch whoever is harvesting the organs whether it be for some sick ritual or for profit, but if that person crossed state lines, we'll have no choice but to involve the FBI."

Rue plugged the coffee machine with quarters. "We've got a full day ahead of us. We need to view what was caught on camera between Congress and Whitaker along with interviewing those animal abusers."

"I'm sure Royce will have Bentley and Lawrence take half that workload. Makes no difference to me which half either."

Rue huffed. "I'm sick of looking at footage. I'd rather get up in the faces of those sickos and see what they have to say."

I chuckled. "That does sound entertaining."

With our coffees in hand, we headed down to the briefing room. Vice was going to sit in on the meeting to offer their assistance if needed.

Once everyone was seated, Bleu approached the podium. He began with the overnight work that had taken place after yesterday's update from Sergeant Riley.

"I need everyone's attention. I assume the water-cooler talk already took place this morning and everyone knows about the unfortunate tragedy involving Valerie

Dawson. We need to nip this case in the bud before the people of Savannah go into a citywide panic. Between the weekend shift and our night shift people, we've narrowed down the last time illegal organ trafficking was discovered in the South. That was in 2007 in Atlanta, and the participants are all behind bars. Either this is a ritualistic ceremony, somebody new who's trying their hand at harvesting organs for profit, or the worst-case scenario, people who have been busy at it but have never been caught."

Royce spoke up. "Cannon and Rue, pass those camera locations off to Bentley and Lawrence. You found the cameras yesterday, so they can follow up with them." He looked at me. "Plus, you'd probably like to give your leg a break. I want the two of you to track down the animal abusers and see what and who they know. After we see if there is any usable video footage to follow up with, or if we get leads from those freaks with the arrest records for animal abuse, we'll decide if we need to overlap shifts."

I nodded a thanks to Royce. A short question-and-answer session between the sergeants and the police squad took place, then the briefing was adjourned. Rue and I headed upstairs to get the current addresses of those four worst offenders, and we would pay them a visit that morning.

Before we left, we made a stop in Lawrence and Bentley's office. We passed along the locations of the cameras and wished them luck. If the cameras were programmed to run twenty-four hours a day, at least a few of them had to have picked up Valerie walking by. If any vehicle seemed to be following her, they needed to get the best angle of that vehicle they could.

Rue and I headed to the apartment of Jacob Kenney, an alleged leader of a cultlike group that partook in many animal sacrifices, even large animals, according to the police reports. His rap sheet was disturbing. He'd spent plenty of time in jail over the last ten years, but most recently, he'd been lying low. I wondered whether he'd changed his evil ways or just become more cunning and clever at hiding his actions.

We reached the apartment building, which had seen better days, at nine o'clock, a time when most unemployed losers were just getting up. Perfect for us, not so perfect for him. We'd checked his most current DMV file as we had with the other three as well. His address was up to date, and the vehicle on record was a 2011 Ford Econoline van. It didn't take much imagination to figure out why he had that vehicle. He transported either like-minded animal abusers or possibly the dead animals themselves. I'd never met the man, but already, he gave me the creeps.

I pulled in and parked in one of the two visitor spaces then scanned from left to right. I pointed at the white Ford van at the end of the lot. "Looks like he's home."

Devon huffed. "Good. Let's go shake his tree and see what kind of nut falls out."

We walked to his door, and I gave it three hard raps. Minutes later, the blinds separated, and a set of eyeballs peered out at us. He looked to be deciding what to do, but since it was obvious that we saw him, he came to the door.

By his appearance, it wasn't too much of a stretch to assume we woke him, and he didn't look happy.

"Yeah?" He scratched his armpit, sniffed his fingers, then looked us up and down.

I held out my badge. "We're detectives from the Habersham precinct and have questions for you. May we come in?"

He wrinkled his face. "What if I say no?"

"Then you'll answer our questions at the station. Either way, we're going to ask them."

He groaned. "Whatever." He jerked his head toward the living room, and we walked in. "What's this about?"

"Why don't you take a seat, listen to what we have to say, and then you can answer the questions?"

Jacob plopped down on the couch and lit a cigarette.

I glanced at Rue, rolled my eyes, and began. "We've looked over your police record and see that you've got a fascination for torturing, killing, and sacrificing innocent animals."

He blew out a puff of smoke then chuckled.

I frowned. "Why is that funny?"

"That was ages ago, and I served my time for it. I'm a changed man, so why are you really here?"

"I'll be honest. We need information, and if you're really a changed man, you'll help," I said.

That time, he laughed. "So it's time to turn the screws and apply pressure, huh? Don't take me for an idiot, Detective…"

"Cannon, Mitch Cannon."

He let out a long, dramatic sigh and frowned at the clock. "I have better things to do, but if you get to the point, I'll answer your questions. You've got fifteen minutes, and your time starts now."

I wanted to strangle the pompous jerk, but to glean information from him, I had to play his game. "Sure, and it shouldn't take longer than that unless there are things you want to tell us about yourself."

His eyes lit up. I knew from past experience that no

matter how large, small, or sick their crimes were, criminals loved to talk about themselves.

He lit a second cigarette, sucked in a long drag, and blew it toward us. "Yeah, okay. Shoot."

Chapter 10

I was pretty certain that our question-and-answer session would last more than fifteen minutes. Once Jacob had the opportunity to gloat and deem himself worthy of being listened to, a lengthy self-absorbed story would begin. At least, his arrogant personality made me think that. Our questions needed to be answered first, then he could talk all he wanted.

I sat back and continued. "During the time you abused and sacrificed animals, what was the largest animal you killed?"

"Strange question, but a cow. Sacrificing cows has been around for centuries along with goats and sheep."

"And you killed them too?"

"Yeah."

"Why?"

"It was part of our"—he air-quoted the word—"ceremony."

I cleared my throat and continued. "A satanic ceremony is what you mean to say, right? The police report says you boasted about being the leader of a cult."

"We had our own religion. First Amendment thing, you know? Anyone can practice or even invent their own religion, even if others call it a cult. A number of well-publicized religions come to mind." He glanced at the clock again. "Why don't you get to the real point?"

The man irritated me more with every passing minute. I tipped my head at Rue, and he took over.

"Did you know anyone back then who sacrificed or currently sacrifices living, breathing people in their ceremonies?"

Jacob's eyes widened, and he grinned. I felt like slapping that grin off his face. It was obvious that he enjoyed that type of question. He rubbed his hands together. "Now we're getting down to the nitty-gritty. So, somebody is sacrificing people in Savannah, huh? That's some wild shit."

I interrupted his elation. "I'm sure you're enjoying this, but we don't need your personal opinion. We need names of anyone now or in the past who has done that, whether it's in Savannah, the county, or the state."

"Hmm…" He rubbed his chin and appeared to be thinking.

I stood. I'd had enough of his taunts. "Obviously, you don't know shit. Guess you weren't the big cult leader you tried to portray."

"Hey, wait. I didn't give you an answer yet."

"And our time is almost up. Do you have names or not?"

"Depends."

I groaned. "On what?"

"On what you mean by sacrificing. Isn't simple murder a way of sacrificing?"

Rue cut in. "There's nothing simple about murder, especially for the victim and their family. We're talking about removing human organs to sacrifice, eat, worship, or rub all over your body. You name it. So, do you know anyone who has done that?"

He shrugged. "Can't say that I do."

"Can't say or won't say?" I asked.

"That was a long time ago, and we smoked a lot of weird shit. My mind is foggy about what went down at those ceremonies and who did what."

I pulled open the door and stepped outside. "Like I said before, you obviously weren't the big man you led people to believe you were."

Rue took up the rear, and we left.

I grumbled as we headed to the cruiser. "Why do jerks like him think so little of life? Everything was a joke to him."

Rue swatted the air. "Don't give that ass a second thought. He must have been a real jerk ten years ago, too, and it's apparent he hasn't changed. Time to move on to the next person."

We drove to the next closest house, one that belonged to Lance Green. His crimes were similar to Jacob's but hadn't occurred quite as frequently. Torturing and killing animals sickened me, especially as much as I loved Gus, and I couldn't fathom somebody doing something so heinous to an innocent pet. I already despised the man, and I hadn't even met him yet.

We reached the house, and I slid into an open curb spot one property away. After walking to the door, I banged on it twice. Since there wasn't a garage and no car was parked directly in front of the house, we had no idea whether he was home or not. After five minutes of knocking, I chalked it up to the guy not being there and made a note to check back on another day.

The third person on the list lived on East Henry near

the Carnegie Library. The drive took only five minutes. Again, we walked to the front door, knocked, and waited. A minute later, the door swung open, but the person standing there wasn't who I'd expected to see. We'd double-checked all addresses on the DMV website, and Dan Clayton's was confirmed. His, like the others, was current, yet an older woman stood there as if waiting for us to say something.

"Hello, ma'am. We're Detectives Cannon and Rue from the Habersham precinct."

"Yes? What can I help you with?"

"Is this your home, ma'am?"

She frowned. "Well, that's a stupid question. Would I be here answering the door if it wasn't my home?"

"We aren't quite sure. Does a Daniel Clayton live here?"

"He does. He's my grandson. Why?"

"We need to have a word with him, so would you mind calling him out here?"

"No, I wouldn't mind, but he isn't home." She wedged her hand into her hip and waited.

She had a way of making me uncomfortable. Whether that was deliberate or not, I didn't know. "Do you know where he is?"

"Nope. He doesn't report to me. He said he'd be gone for a week or so, and then he up and left."

I pulled my notepad and pen out of my inner sport jacket pocket and wrote that down. "What day exactly did he leave home?"

"Saturday night."

"And he didn't say where he was going?"

"That's what I said."

Rue took over. "Was his leaving planned?"

She chuckled. "Obviously, it was to him. Otherwise,

he'd still be here. Did I know about it? Nope, I sure didn't. Sometimes, it's nice to have a quiet, clean house, though, if you know what I mean. Is there anything else?"

"Did he say what day he was returning?" Rue asked.

She shook her head. "Don't you folks listen? He said he'd be gone a week or so."

I sighed. We wouldn't get anything more out of her. It seemed she was being deliberately evasive. "Okay, thank you, ma'am." I handed her my card and told her to call when he returned but knew she would crumple it up and throw it away as soon as we walked out the door.

Back in the car, I groaned in disgust. "Why is it so hard for people to cooperate? Why play the guessing games?"

"Because it's their family and they don't want to share information with the police. We're the bad guys, remember?" Rue said.

"Whatever. Don't you think it's a bit convenient that Mr. Clayton suddenly left town about the same time Valerie was dumped in the marsh?"

"Yep, and that's why Daniel Clayton just moved up to the top position on our person-of-interest list."

I unfolded the sheet of paper that was lying in the cup holder. "Okay, one more name, and then it's back to the drawing board."

"So, where are we headed now?"

"Would you believe only a few blocks from the street Valerie lived on?"

"Humph. That could be something. Maybe the guy knew her."

I nodded. "Maybe, so let's go find out."

We reached Tim Grandon's house, parked and headed up the sidewalk, and I gave the door a knock. By then, it was after ten o'clock. Anyone who wasn't extremely lazy or worked the graveyard shift would be up and around by that time of day. Seconds later, a face peered out between the drawn curtains. He was home and awake. I knocked again, not giving him too much time to decide whether he was going to answer the door or not. I watched the doorknob, and it finally turned. It was obvious by the lack of footsteps sounding on the floor that he was in socks or barefoot and possibly hadn't left the house yet that morning.

The door opened about a foot, and he stared out at us. "If you're going to preach to me, I'm not interested."

"We're detectives," I said, "not evangelical zealots."

"What do you want?"

"To talk to you. That's obviously the reason we're here, unless you aren't Tim Grandon. Are you?"

He nodded and opened the door farther. "What is this about? I haven't caused any mischief for a good year now."

"We don't care about that," I said. "We're looking for information."

"About what?"

"About the activity you used to participate in."

"But—"

"Don't worry. We aren't here to bust your balls. You've served your time"—I cocked my head—"and don't do foolish things like that anymore, right?"

"That's what I said."

"So, we need to know about the people you used to associate with who may still be into that type of thing. Voodoo, animal sacrifices, weird cult shit, you know. Anyone come to mind?"

Tim grumbled. "I keep to myself."

"But those things still go on, don't they? Behind

closed doors, out in the woods, inside abandoned buildings."

I stared into his eyes. His face told me he was uncomfortable. He looked at the floor and jammed his hands into his pockets.

"I suppose so, but I mind my own business."

Rue took over. "And that's good, but I'm sure you remember some of those names, and we need them. Do the right thing, Tim, and tell us."

I tipped my head toward the couch, indicating that he should sit. He did, then Rue pulled out his notepad, and we listened.

"I didn't know a lot of people, only the ones that were part of my clan."

"Clan? That's what you called it?"

"Yeah. We didn't use the word 'cult,' but it was more or less the same thing."

"How many people were in your clan, and why weren't all of them arrested when you were?" I asked.

He shrugged. "Anywhere between ten and fifteen people, and the reason everyone wasn't arrested is because the ones who squealed out the others first got the deal. They gave names, we were arrested, and they got off scot-free."

"Why not arrest everyone?"

"Because the cops didn't know who we were. Everyone scattered when they rolled in, and only a handful of guys were caught."

Rue nodded. "Gotcha. So are some still practicing animal sacrifices for the clan?"

"I've heard things. Whether they're true or not, I don't know."

I cocked my head. "Like?"

"Like Dylan Marx, Joey Nisbett, Trent Fremont, and a few others started that shit up again."

I raised my brows. "Recently?"

Tim nodded.

"Has anyone gone further than that?"

He frowned at me. "I don't know what you mean."

"What I mean is that we found a dead woman with her organs removed. Let's not beat around the bush, Tim. Who is the sketchiest person you know, and would they do something like that?"

I was tired of getting the runaround from people. They'd either heard of someone or knew someone who might have advanced to eating human organs or sacrificing them.

"I've never—"

"Yeah, yeah. Nobody has ever known someone who took that leap. But if you did, who would they be?"

He hesitated, likely weighing his options. "If I give you a few names, will I remain anonymous?"

"Absolutely," I said. "I give you my word."

Chapter 11

Normally, I wouldn't give my word to anyone unless I intended to keep it. I didn't see a reason to backpedal now. We would interview the people whose names Tim gave us, and that would be that. There wasn't a good reason to disclose his name, and it wouldn't serve any useful purpose.

Devon waited with pen in hand for Tim to give us the names of those he thought might go to the extreme of human sacrifice. On our own, we didn't have a single name, but with his help, we would compare the names to the rest of those nine police jackets we had.

Reluctantly, he told us that Dylan Marx and Trent Fremont would likely go that far if one was coaxed by the other. "They were as thick as thieves and usually the two who initiated every animal kill and sacrifice. The rest of us were as stupid as sheep."

"And I imagine sheep were also sacrificed," I said sarcastically.

Tim stared at the floor again. "Yeah, they were."

I handed him my card. "Okay, and that's all you know?"

"It is."

"Thanks, and if you think of any more names, just call."

"I won't."

I frowned since I wasn't sure exactly what he meant. Maybe he wouldn't come up with more names, or maybe he wouldn't call if he did. No matter what, we knew where he lived if we had to go back and talk to him again.

Rue and I returned to the precinct with the little information we'd gotten. We'd interviewed only two of the four people we'd intended to, and only one had told us anything. We had a twenty-five percent success rate on that trip—not the best. So far, only Tim had given us a few names to work with, although even that wasn't voluntary.

We checked for Dylan and Trent's names in that group of nine that had been arrested for animal abuse years earlier. Their names weren't among them. That worried me. Had twisted people like them slipped through the cracks? Were they currently committing heinous deeds right in Savannah's backyard? We needed to find out.

After buying two coffees, we returned to our office and prepared to find out more on the two names we'd gotten. Before I forgot, I grabbed my phone to call Royce and ask whether Lawrence and Bentley had reported in yet. If luck and the right camera angle were on our side, they might have seen Valerie walking to her car, a suspicious vehicle following her, or even the abduction itself.

"Hey, Boss, Rue and I are back with a little information to follow up on."

"At least that's something," Royce said.

"Nothing back from Bentley and Lawrence on the cameras?"

"They saw Valerie on Sparky's outdoor camera, which only caught her for a half block. Then they saw her again near the intersection at Whitaker as she turned south. No further reports since then, and that was an hour ago."

"Okay, just wondering. We're going to look up those two names, grab lunch, and then check out the rest of the abusers who have police records." I ended the call and joggled my computer's mouse, and the screen came to life. Rue looked up Trent Fremont on his computer, and I entered the name Dylan Marx on mine. As I waited for the program to propagate, I tapped my fingers against the desk. When the results popped up, I leaned in closer and read them. "Humph."

Rue glanced across his desk. "What does 'humph' mean?"

"Looks like Dylan Marx has a lengthy arrest record."

Rue perked up. "Yeah, for what?"

"You name it, but nothing that sent him away for more than a year. Battery on men and women, selling weed, breaking and entering, forging checks, and holding an ex-girlfriend in his house against her will."

"And none of that ever got him more than a year in the joint?"

"Nope. His attorney always bargained the sentence down."

"Humph," Rue said. "Lucky guy."

"Let's put him on the person of interest list along

with Daniel Clayton and then speak to the rest of the nine." I sighed. "It'll take the remainder of the day, and after that, we should know which direction this investigation is going to take us."

"Meaning whether Valerie was killed for profit or for sacrifice?"

"That's exactly right."

Seconds later, my desk phone rang. Royce was on the other end. I answered and pressed Speaker so Rue could listen in.

"Cannon, I just got word from Bentley. He said they finished reviewing every camera along Valerie's route. They didn't see a vehicle follow her or anyone abduct her. The last camera was too far away from where her heel was found to catch anything."

That much, I was relatively sure of considering the distance that last store camera was from her high heel.

"Damn it. So we really don't know if she was dragged away or picked up in a vehicle."

"That's correct."

I let out an involuntary groan. "That doesn't leave us with much, but we'll continue down the path we're taking now. Maybe Bentley and Lawrence can pitch in with interviewing the remaining animal abusers. If each of them gives us a new name, we might get somewhere."

"Yep, continue with what you're doing, and I'll have the guys stop in your office when they get back."

"Roger that." I turned to Rue after hanging up. "Get anything on Trent?"

Rue rubbed his chin. "Still reading, but he sure as hell isn't a Sunday school teacher. Looks like he just got a visit from the PD last week."

"Really? Why?"

"Neighbor called it in. Said he was threatening to poison her dog."

"Did he say why?"

"Yeah, he doesn't like animals."

Chapter 12

The doorbell rang, and Chase rose to answer it. "Finally, geez. The pizza is probably cold by now."

Teddy temporarily covered the money that was sitting on the coffee table with a couch throw, then he went to the kitchen and pulled two cans of beer from the fridge. He heard a few seconds of conversation, then the door closed. The coast was clear to remove the throw and enjoy staring at all that cash while they ate their pizza.

Chase jerked his head at the coffee table. "Make room for the pizza boxes then grab a couple of plates and some paper towels."

Teddy did as told, not out of fear but simply because Chase was the eldest brother, and that was the way their life had always been. The younger did what the older brother said.

After they each had a slice of pizza on their plate and an open beer at their side, they resumed staring at the stacks of cash that lay in front of them.

Chase pointed his chin at the money. "Have you ever

made that kind of money in your life for something so easy?"

Teddy huffed. "That was rhetorical, right?"

Together they laughed, knowing full well that up to that point, they'd both lived simple lifestyles.

"We can quit our dead-end jobs and harvest a few more organs over the next week or two. After that—"

"We'll do what?" Teddy asked.

"Buy that boat we've been talking about. Hell, we can buy a fishing boat and a boat to show off like the weekend jackasses do on the river."

Teddy chuckled. "First, you've already quit your dead-end job, and second, we can buy that big boat, take it out to Hilton Head, and show off to the folks and their hotshot friends."

Chase rose and walked into the kitchen, where he grabbed two more beers then returned to the couch. "Nah, we can't do that. They'd ask too many questions, plus they don't give a shit about us anyway."

Teddy's forehead wrinkled. "Well, what's the fun of having cool shit if we can't show it off? We'll say you won the lottery or something."

"Let's worry about the folks later." Chase grinned. "We haven't even picked out a boat yet. For now, we have to find our next organ donor."

Teddy glanced at the clock. "I have to go into work for a few hours, but you can drop me off. We'll sidetrack past the mall and see how many ladies walk out to their cars alone."

"You want to do something in broad daylight? That's super risky."

"We can look, can't we? A strategic plan takes a day or so to form, but we can surveil the place now and see what we think. We'd have to park at the far end of the lot where the cameras can't pick us up and next to a high-end car. Well-off people are the only ones who care about door dingers. They park their expensive cars as far away from everyone else as they can."

"Right, but it's probably the fifty-year-old wife of a CEO, who has never lifted a finger in her life except to carry shopping bags from the pricey stores out to her pricey car."

Teddy shrugged. "Yeah, so what? She'd be easy to overtake. Once the organs are out of the body, nobody knows the age of the donor."

Chase smiled. "True enough."

They clinked beer cans, guzzled the golden brew, and grabbed another slice of pizza.

Thirty minutes later, the brothers left the house and headed to the mall on the south end of town. Teddy drove since he knew the area better and the mall was relatively new. It took all of fifteen minutes before he was trolling the parking lot while looking for the perfect place to park.

"Damn, this place is huge," Chase said.

"Yep, and I bet there are a lot of women shoppers inside."

"Seems like this occupation suits you, brother."

Teddy grinned. "A lot of money suits me. I'm going to drive along the edges of the lot. It's safer there, being out of camera range, and when the time comes, nobody will see us snatch our next organ donor. That person's car will be parked next to the sliding door, so even if the cameras did reach that far out in the lot, the body of the van would hide the activity going on. Everything will happen on the other side."

Chase cocked his head as he took in Teddy's idea. "That's pretty damn smart if I do say so myself. Okay,

I'm on board. Let's find the right car and see what happens."

Within a few minutes, Teddy pointed out the window. "That's what I'm talking about. See those two women who just got out of that Audi?"

Chase looked in the same direction as his brother.

"They're going into the store, but at some point and likely with their hands full, they'll come out and load the trunk or back seat, all while they're busy talking about their purchases. They wouldn't even notice us about to grab them."

"But that's just an example since we wouldn't snatch two at once."

"Right. We can't press our luck, but something like that can't be too hard to do."

Chase agreed. "So what's your work schedule for the week?"

Chapter 13

Rue and I had Dylan and Trent to check out as well as Lance Green, the person who hadn't answered his door earlier. We would bang on his door one more time today. If we didn't have luck the second time, we'd get a unit to sit on his house to see whether he really wasn't home or had just chosen to ignore our presence.

I handed off the files of the remaining people with police records to Bentley and Lawrence for them to interview. We'd likely exhaust those few names without learning anything promising, yet there was the chance of getting additional names from those folks. I assumed it would be a process of elimination until we'd spoken to all current and past animal abusers that we knew of. If the same name was mentioned by several people, we would focus on that person.

Even though we were Homicide, our job still involved a lot of legwork, phone calls, interviews, and luck to make sure the right person landed behind bars. We were used to it, and although it seemed we were spinning our wheels at times, we usually ended up with the perp right where he was destined to be, in either a prison cell or, sometimes, a coffin.

We headed out again after lunch, that time to interview Trent and Dylan. Lance Green was scheduled after that. For all we knew, the guy might have a legitimate job that he'd been at earlier.

We reached Dylan's apartment just after two o'clock. It never failed to amaze me how everyday criminals could have the same conveniences that hardworking people had, yet most of them didn't work for a living. I imagined the "jobs" they did have weren't the type that could be reported to the IRS.

Our database showed Dylan lived on the first floor of an apartment building on the west side of Savannah. Not the best neighborhood but a good one for drug trafficking if that was something he did for a living.

I turned onto Brewer Street then parked, and we headed up the sidewalk to building number six. His apartment was on the left corner. The music coming from inside made my knocks go unheard. I pounded harder until the music stopped and someone swung open the door. Staring out at us was a twentysomething woman with dyed-blond hair with black roots. Her hair was piled on top of her head in a bird's nest fashion. She wore the shortest shorts I'd ever seen and a white tank top. On her shoulder, a tattoo of a large spider finished off her strange look. She smacked her gum while she gave us the once-over.

"Yeah?"

"Is Dylan Marx here?"

"Who's asking?"

Rue held out his badge. "The cops. So, is he here or not?"

"Yeah, yeah. Don't get your panties in a bundle. He's in the shower."

I jerked my chin toward the hallway. "Go get him."

She rolled her eyes and walked away.

I shook my head. "I've nearly reached my daily limit of smart-ass people." My eyes bulged when Dylan came from the hallway, still dripping wet with a towel wrapped around his waist.

"What do you want?" he asked.

"What I want is for you to put on your clothes and then come back here. We've got questions for you."

He snarled at us. "About?"

"About your past and current hobbies. Now go."

It took a good five minutes before he returned to the living room. At least he was dressed that time. He looked around.

"Where's Daisy?"

I furrowed my brows. "Is that the girl or the cat that just scurried by?"

"Real funny. It's the girl."

"She opened the slider and wandered off outside. So, Dylan, we need to know what you've been up to lately."

"Why?"

"Because your name was mentioned in a conversation about animal-sacrifice rituals. You doing that type of thing?"

He smiled. "Of course not."

I didn't expect him to admit his actions, and we had no way to prove he was involved in any current illegal activity unless we shadowed his every move. I wanted to focus on the fact that we were after the person who'd killed Valerie Dawson and removed her organs. Our job wasn't to bust a bunch of people conducting weird ceremonial rituals—not our department—yet we needed names.

"Do you know anyone who is? Is there a cult leader with a following who is working areas of Savannah?"

"You're asking the wrong person. Go talk to Jacob Kenney."

I played dumb. "Jacob Kenney, huh? Who the heck is he?"

"He's the grand pooh-bah, the king of kings, the cult leader. Call him what you like, but if anyone is active and recruiting followers, it's him."

"So he's a friend of yours?"

"I know him from a past life, but I don't participate in that stuff anymore."

Rue huffed. "Funny how everyone says the same thing."

My gut told me we weren't going to get anywhere with the interviews. Nobody would admit anything, and without us witnessing the act itself, our hours spent with those morons would be a waste of time. We needed the people calling the shots, the ones in charge. They were the most demented. Dylan and Jacob fit the bill, yet they'd slithered out of our questions like snakes and sent us on wild-goose chases that ended with little or no information. I knew we were being played—likely by both of them.

Rue and I returned to the precinct. We would see if Lawrence and Bentley had had better luck than we did, but I had my doubts. People threw out names to deflect the focus from them, then the new people we talked to did the same thing. For now, the only two I was interested in were Dylan Marx and Jacob Kenney. Especially since Dylan knew Jacob's name, it seemed they were the leaders of Savannah's cult activity—if there actually was any.

Lawrence and Bentley were back. They said they hadn't had any success, and as long as Vice hadn't gotten word of new animal-abuse activity and hadn't made any arrests, we had nothing but snickers and smart remarks from the people we'd interviewed. The only one who seemed forthright was Tim, yet the names he gave us got us nowhere.

I needed to talk to Royce, and a fresh cup of coffee sounded good. The cafeteria was on my way to his office anyway.

I knocked twice, and he yelled out to come in. I peered around the door, and he was engrossed in something on his computer. He looked at me, pushed his reading glasses back up on his nose, and asked what I needed.

"A minute of your time if you have it to spare."

With a groan, he stretched, removed his glasses, and squeezed the sides of his nose. "Go ahead. Shoot."

"Well, we've had zero success with the interviews, and Lance Green still isn't home. The people we've spoken with either clam up, treat our questions like jokes, don't know anything, or point us toward somebody else who doesn't know anything either. Better yet, those people point the finger back at the person we just interviewed."

"Humph."

"Vice would know if a new group of 'sacrificial worshippers' popped up, wouldn't they?"

"I'd think so. They're in charge of weeding out the real threats, whether it's animal abuse, human abuse, or anything in between. So, do you have a different approach, or don't you think they're involved at all?"

I shook my head. "At this point, I don't know a damn thing. Is it overstepping to involve the FBI now?"

"Yeah, it is. We have nothing that says a person of interest in our jurisdiction, which we don't have said person, committed a crime that took them over county let alone state lines."

"What about asking questions?"

"You mean if the FBI has heard of or knows of illegal organ trafficking that's currently going on?"

"Yeah, that. We need to know which tree to bark up before we can actually work the case."

Royce scratched the stubble on his chin. "I guess you have a point. Okay, I'll call the nearest field office and have them make a contact. I don't want to go over anyone's head or step on toes. We can't end up on their bad side since we may be working this case side by side with them a week from now."

I stood and headed for the door. "Boss?"

"Yep."

"We do have a few FBI friends. The ones who were here last year when we had that K2 resurgence."

"Right. I nearly forgot. I bet they'd talk to us off the record." Royce tapped his computer keys. "What the hell were their names?"

"Jade Monroe and Lorenzo DeLeon. I have both of their contact cards in my desk drawer."

"Okay, call me with those numbers. I'll let you know what I find out after I talk to them. Give me a half hour."

"Thanks, Boss."

After buying my coffee, I headed to our office, feeling like this case was going to be tougher to solve than I'd thought. If there was actually a criminal investigation of organ trafficking going on somewhere in the United

States, I had a feeling the case would be scooped up by the FBI and added to whatever they already had, even if it wasn't related. I'd get Rue to field a few questions and get his opinions. Was it human organ sacrifice or human organ sales? I thought it could go either way.

When I returned, our office was empty. Rue was likely going over something with Bentley and Lawrence, so I took that time to call Royce and give him the phone numbers. Now, we waited. Rue walked in minutes later with snacks. I didn't have to ask where he'd gone.

"How did I miss you in the hallway?" I asked.

"Made a stop in the bathroom first."

I nodded. While I waited for Royce's call, I was digging deeper into Jacob and Dylan's backgrounds, which gave me more information on their personalities and twisted behaviors. Both men were career criminals, regardless of whether their crimes were serious or petty. They'd never landed in the slammer for any length of time. Yet they were dangerous in the sense that they were unpredictable and willing to do nearly anything if it suited the situation or benefited them in the long run.

I rolled my neck and heard it crack. Rue frowned.

"Stiff neck?"

"Yeah, I guess."

"That's a sign of stress."

I chuckled. "Really? I had no idea."

"So, what's bothering you?"

"Other than killing and gutting a human being? Tell me your take on this investigation, Rue. Where do you see it going?"

Devon let out a hard sigh. "You mean do I think the religious cult nutjobs are responsible?"

"Yeah, or do you think Valerie was killed by someone who wanted to profit off her organs?"

"Tapper did say her organs were removed carefully so as not to damage them."

"He used those actual words?"

Rue swatted the air. "I'm paraphrasing, Mitch, but to me, those idiots we interviewed earlier don't seem that smart. In my opinion, they'd tend to be the type who'd pull out organs like a hunter, without too much care or caution."

My nod spoke for me. I had to agree with Devon's assessment.

"I asked Royce to call the FBI for information. We do have a few friends in the bureau who might be willing to share what they know with us. If anyone would know about illegal organ sales going on now or in the last year or so, it would be Jade and Renz. Royce said he'd make the call. He also said it was too soon to get them involved since we don't even have a suspect."

"Makes sense. So he's going to contact them specifically?"

"Yep, and it'll be interesting to find out what they say." I shook my head. "The problem with the FBI is that they'll keep an eye on our progress and then swoop in and claim the victory."

Rue huffed. "Unfortunately, that sounds pretty accurate."

Chapter 14

The phone call I'd been waiting for finally came. I yanked the receiver toward me and answered. "Cannon here."

"Mitch, I talked to Lorenzo DeLeon. What he told me didn't help much."

I let out an involuntary sigh, and my shoulders slumped. "So, what did he say?"

"He said there were active cases in several states throughout the US but that he and Jade weren't working them. The bureaus in LA and New York handled those two known investigations because they remained within the state. If anything has crossed state lines or become part of the organized crime syndicate, he hasn't been made privy to it yet."

"Hmm. Well, that's no help to us. So there has been organ trafficking going on in New York and California, and was that recent?"

"He said in the last eight months. The people involved in both states are sitting in jail, and if it's still going on or has spread to other locations, they haven't caught wind of it yet."

"Okay, but that sounds like the door has been left open for that possibility."

"It does sound that way. For now, both of you go home. Tell Bentley and Lawrence to do the same. We're going to have a multidepartment brainstorming session in the morning."

"Roger that. Night, Boss."

"Good night, Mitch."

I placed the receiver back on the base. I was sure a look of disappointment had spread across my face, and Rue obviously noticed.

"So nothing helpful?"

"Nope, and we can't just sit on Dylan and Jacob's houses since we don't have evidence of either of them committing a crime." I grabbed my sport jacket off the wall hook. "Come on over for a bit. I'm sure we can both use a beer."

"Sure. You don't have to ask me twice."

Rue and I left for my house. I gave Marie a quick call to let her know he was coming over. She said he was more than welcome to stay for supper. There was plenty of spaghetti to go around.

Once we arrived home, I let Devon know what was on the menu and asked if he wanted to stay. His grin was all the answer I needed.

"Just an FYI, we'll talk about the case after supper while we enjoy that beer out on the deck. No shop talk in front of the kids."

Rue chuckled. "No worries. My mouth will be preoccupied with eating anyway."

Our supper conversation was mostly centered on what the girls had been doing during their summer break. Rue also made sure to ask Mom what she had been doing to entertain herself. She was happy to report that she and Marie were making pebble art on a daily basis but also that they'd been doing a lot of baking.

I rubbed my belly as if I'd been regularly enjoying too many sweets, and Mom offered to send Rue home later with a container of chocolate chip cookies.

"I guess I can't refuse that," Rue said. "It would be rude."

The girls giggled then helped Marie clear the table.

With a head tip toward the deck and two cold bottles of beer in hand, I led the way outside. Rue and I would talk shop for a bit before calling it a night.

I dropped down on one of the four Adirondack chairs and placed my beer on the wide arm.

"How are we going to figure this out, Rue? There isn't an actual video of Valerie being abducted or showing where they kept her for a full day or where she was killed. All we know is that she disappeared after the bars closed early Saturday morning and was discovered dead out in the marsh on Sunday. The time in between is a blank."

Rue groaned. "I don't even want to imagine what she likely went through, but if it was a cult sacrifice, it must have taken place late Saturday night. That's the only way Tapper's TOD timeline would make sense. They killed her, did their crazy sacrifice thing, and then dumped her body before daylight broke."

"Right, or the exact same scenario took place except the cult ritual didn't happen. Whoever gutted her sold off her organs within hours of killing her and then dumped her remains the same way. It literally could go either way."

"And that means we have to figure out which one it was in order to pursue the people involved," Rue said.

I took a gulp of beer. "And that isn't going to be easy."

After we'd had an hour of discussing the case and a second beer, Rue left. Tomorrow was another workday, and it was nearly nine o'clock.

I returned to the house and saw that the girls had gone upstairs, and Mom and Marie were watching TV. I sat with them and mindlessly watched the program they seemed to be enjoying. The news would come on next, and that made me wonder if there was anything we could air to help the case. I planned to discuss that possibility at our brainstorming meeting in the morning.

Chapter 15

"What do you think, Chase?"

The elder brother grinned. "It would be risky, and I'd have to make sure that one of my contacts needed organs that quickly—"

Teddy interrupted. "Not as risky as it would be during the daytime, and what contact wouldn't want organs on a regular basis? They have plenty of buyers, and it's a shit ton of money in everyone's pockets." Teddy pointed at the cell phone lying on the coffee table. "Make some calls. We have an hour before the mall closes."

Chase tapped the phone's keys, spoke to several people, while Teddy listened in on his brother's side of the conversation. A thumbs-up told him it was a go.

Chase hung up after the third call and stood. "It's on, so that means we have to plan this out to the letter. Mr. Harris wants delivery in Augusta by five a.m."

"That's pushing it. We need to wait until the mall closes and the last few people walk out. That's when we'll make our move," Teddy said.

"But there won't be time to bring the woman here, kill her, remove the organs, dump her in the marsh, and drive two and a half hours to Augusta. I'll have to call him back and tell him we can't make the deadline." Chase lifted his phone. "We might lose a customer, though."

"Wait. I have a better idea. Grab the keys, and we'll get the van ready."

At a quarter till ten, the brothers left for the mall. The stage was set. They had everything they needed in the back of the van, and after finding and killing the next victim and removing the organs, they would head directly to Augusta and make it with time to spare.

Teddy found a lone car parked much farther out in the lot than the rest. It wasn't a high-end vehicle, but it did look new.

"There. That car will do just fine," he said as he parked next to an empty space. They needed room between the van and the chosen vehicle to jump out, take the owner by surprise, and disable or kill them immediately. "Now we wait." Teddy grinned at Chase. "It's like fishing, brother. We get that nibble, then we set the hook."

It was ten o'clock, and they watched as people exited the building, walked to their cars, and drove away.

"Come on already," Chase said as the lot cleared.

"Don't worry. The fewer people around, the better for us."

They finally saw two women walk out together and head in their direction.

Chase pounded his fist on the dash. "Damn it. There's two of them!"

"Just hang on," Teddy said. "It looks like they're slowing down at that car in the middle of the lot."

They watched as the trunk lid lifted and bags were placed inside, then the women talked as one climbed in behind the wheel. Minutes later, she drove off, and the other woman continued toward them.

"Ha! Here she comes." Chase rubbed his hands together.

"Settle down, bro. We have to think fast, act even faster, then get the hell out of here. You jump out, stab her, and toss her in the van. Then you'll follow me in her car to that abandoned school on the south side of town. Nobody ever goes out there. We'll harvest her organs, put them on ice, then place what's left of her carcass in the driver's seat of her own car and be on our way." Teddy looked out the blackened windows. "She's thirty feet from the car and with a coffee cup in hand. She'll climb right in, so get ready to jump out."

"I'm ready and can visualize those stacks of cash in our hands. We'll be getting that boat a lot sooner than you think."

"Good. Got your knife?"

Chase grabbed the door handle. "Got it."

"Okay. Ready, set, go!"

Chapter 16

The next morning, we gathered in the briefing room. Royce wanted Vice to sit in on our meeting and give us the profile of a cult member who used animals in their rituals. They had dealt with the likes of them plenty in the past, and I knew Jacob Kenney was well-known to them. What we didn't know was if they'd ever heard of Dylan Marx and if we were even on track in thinking those types might be responsible for Valerie's death.

From what we'd learned, many people who killed animals did it for pleasure. They were the sickos to watch out for. Psychologists had often noted that over time, animal killers progressed into people killers. That much I knew from watching TV documentaries. We were also told that people who took part in sacrificial killings did it only for the ritual, not for the pleasure it gave them.

Royce begged to differ. "Killing is killing, and I'm sure they took some sick pleasure in it. I'm not buying the whole religious-rights-and-beliefs they spew. They're into black magic and weird shit, and I wouldn't be surprised if some of them went beyond that. They cite how animals were religiously sacrificed over centuries, but in my opinion, those crazies just enjoy it."

"Maybe so, Raleigh, but to jump from animal to human sacrifice seems like a stretch," Sergeant Richardson said.

I took my turn. "I know your department is acquainted with Jacob Kenney, but has a Dylan Marx ever come across your radar?"

Richardson scratched his cheek and looked from one detective to the next. "Anybody?"

They shook their heads and shrugged.

"Not familiar with the name, sir," Detective Denning said.

Richardson returned his focus to Royce. "Doesn't look like we know him, Raleigh."

"Okay. His name came up in the interviews."

"We'll definitely check him out for past involvement, though."

"Appreciate it, Ron." Royce tipped his wrist. "I guess that's all we have, then. This murder case is going nowhere fast."

An officer knocked on the half-opened door then stepped into the room. "Excuse me, but I have some-thing urgent to tell Sergeant Royce."

Royce pointed his chin at the officer. "Go ahead. You can say whatever it is in front of the group."

"Sir, a call came in from a groundskeeper who was checking on the abandoned Sullivan School on the south side of Savannah."

"I'm familiar with the place. Go on."

"He saw a car parked behind the last building and went to investigate. A woman was in the driver's seat with her head against the wheel. He assumed she was sleeping and pounded on the window, but she didn't move. He called 911, and Patrol arrived and did the same thing. Finally, they broke the passenger window, unlocked the doors, and went around to the driver's side." The officer stared at his feet.

Royce frowned. "Continue, Officer Lewis. What was wrong with her?"

"Her entire chest cavity was empty, Sergeant."

Royce leapt from his chair, and we followed suit. Shouting and cursing ran rampant. The sergeant swirled his finger above his head. "Text me her name and address." Royce pointed at our homicide unit. "Let's go."

We took the stairs two at a time to our ground floor and out the door to the parking lot. I dove in behind the wheel, Royce sat shotgun, and Rue jumped in the back. In the second cruiser, Lawrence and Bentley took up the rear. During the drive, Royce spent most of his time making calls to Tapper and Forensics. After hanging up, he looked over his shoulder at Devon.

"See who LeAnn Morrison is. That's the name of the woman the car is registered to."

"On it, Boss."

We reached Sullivan School in ten minutes and drove past the buildings until we saw the parked squad cars. The discovery couldn't have been more than a half hour old. Crime scene tape was going up at the driveway entrance, and we were told that a patrol officer had the groundskeeper waiting in his car to talk to us.

After screeching to a stop, we rushed to the woman's vehicle and dipped under the tape that had already secured a twenty-foot perimeter around it. Both the driver and passenger doors were open, and safety glass covered the ground and interior on the passenger side. The body had been leaned back against the driver's seat. The officers admitted they'd lifted the woman's head and sat her upright before they realized what they were looking at. From that moment on, they hadn't touched anything related to the car or the victim.

"Officer Bardon and I immediately backed away from the vehicle once we realized what her condition was, sir," Officer Lorey told Royce after being asked who the first responders were.

"Tell us every single detail from the second you arrived." Royce held up his finger. "Has anyone checked out the groundskeeper yet?"

Bardon responded. "No, sir. We needed to secure the scene and make the call to Homicide first."

Royce called out to Bentley. "You and Lawrence go interview that groundskeeper and do a background check on him as soon as you learn his name."

I watched as Royce yelled out orders. My mind was spinning with uncertainty. Either that woman was here already for whatever reason, possibly to buy drugs, and was opportunistically killed, or she was murdered and gutted somewhere else and the killer drove her vehicle to that spot. First, we needed to know without any doubt that she was indeed LeAnn Morrison, then we would try to make sense of how she got there.

After gloving up, I leaned into the car to look for her purse and phone. We needed to establish her identity.

Royce yelled out again. "Rue, get SVU on the line and have them patch you through to Missing Persons! Find out if a LeAnn Morrison has been reported missing."

I got down on my knees and did everything in my power to avoid looking at the woman, but I couldn't help myself. Her skin was a sickly whitish blue—nearly gray— and the blouse covering her hollow torso had turned black with hours-old blood. I shook my head, looked away, and jammed my arm under the passenger seat. No purse or phone. I looked in the glove box and console and found the same—nothing. I checked the back seat then the trunk. Nothing to identify the woman was there. The only place left was under the driver's seat or in her pockets, but I couldn't go there yet. Forensics and Tapper would go first. It would be a good hour before we had clearance to examine more. I had an idea that could speed things up and headed for Royce.

"Boss, I didn't see anything inside the car that could identify the woman as LeAnn, and of course we can't search her body yet."

Royce cursed. "Or what's left of it."

I agreed and continued with my idea. "I could go to the home on record for this vehicle, see if anyone is there, and ask for LeAnn by name." I grimaced. "It would be best to take a picture of her face for identification's sake."

Royce paced. "Yeah, the family will find out sooner or later anyway if that's her." He looked around. "Where's Rue? He was supposed to see if she was reported missing."

I shielded my eyes and scanned the area. "Here he comes."

Rue approached us and said no one had reported a LeAnn Morrison missing.

"Well, shit. This lady is somebody. She isn't dressed like a vagrant, and from what we can tell, she doesn't look homeless. Her nails are manicured and polished." Royce jerked his head toward our cruiser. "There's time before we'll know anything, so go ahead and pay the homeowner a visit. Rue, you go along too."

"You got it, sir."

Back in our cruiser, we headed to the address on

record. Once there, I parked, and we walked to the front door of a middle-class home in a middle-class neighborhood. I rang the bell, and we waited. With the garage door closed, it was impossible to know whether anyone was home. There wasn't a car parked directly in front along the curb either.

Minutes passed, and nobody came to the door.

"Now what?" Rue asked.

I pointed across the street, where a woman was gardening. "Let's go see what she knows."

We approached the woman and caught her attention by calling out to her. I didn't want to come up from behind and startle her. "Excuse us, ma'am."

She looked over her shoulder, stood, then removed her gardening gloves. "Yes, may I help you?"

"I sure hope so." I showed her my badge then pointed at the house we'd just left. "Do the Morrisons live there?"

"Yes, Mark and LeAnn."

"Have you seen either of them this morning?"

"I imagine LeAnn already went to work, and I believe Mark is away on business. Is there something I can help you with?"

Her comment about the husband being gone could explain why nobody had reported LeAnn missing. "Can you describe LeAnn to us?"

"That's an odd question, and you can call me Joyce."

"Thank you, Joyce." I waited.

"Well, LeAnn is around forty, I guess, although I've never asked her age. She's pretty and has shoulder-length brown hair."

So far, Joyce's description was matching the woman in the car.

"What would you say she weighs?"

"Um, around one hundred twenty pounds. You know, average weight."

"Do you have Mark's phone number, Joyce?" Rue asked.

"No, sorry, but if you want to talk to LeAnn, I know where she works."

"Great, and where's that?"

"At Flapjack's. It's the pancake house across the street from the new mall. She works there until noon, then later in the day, she works part-time at one of the shoe stores inside the mall."

"So she works morning hours at Flapjack's and goes to the mall later?" I confirmed.

"Yep. Not every day, of course, but probably four days a week. She works until the mall closes at night."

"Thank you for the help. We'll head over to Flap-jack's right now."

We left before she could ask questions. Until the woman in the car was identified, we couldn't assume she was LeAnn or announce it to anyone other than her husband.

Flapjack's was three miles southeast of the Morrison house, only a couple of minutes away. We arrived to a full restaurant—nine thirty was prime breakfast time. The young lady behind the hostess stand said there was a fifteen-minute wait.

Leaning in closer so the people around us didn't overhear, I told the hostess we were detectives and needed to speak with the manager right away. I also asked if LeAnn had shown up for work that morning.

Her headshake was all the answer I needed.

"I'll get the manager. Give me a minute, please."

Rue and I stepped out of line and watched for someone to come down the hallway. Less than a minute later, a man and the hostess walked in our direction. She pointed at us then returned to the hostess stand. The man approached Rue and me and introduced himself as David Conn.

"May we talk somewhere privately?" I asked as I looked at the crowded entryway. "It's kind of loud out here."

"Sure thing. We'll talk in my office. Right this way."

Chapter 17

Mr. Conn offered us the guest chairs, and we sat down with a thank-you nod. He took a seat at his desk, folded his hands, and looked concerned.

"Lisa said you asked about LeAnn Morrison."

I took the lead. "Yes, we did. We're assuming LeAnn didn't show up for work this morning."

"That's right, she didn't, and that isn't typical of her. LeAnn is very responsible. We tried her phone several times, but it just went to voicemail."

"Do you have any photos of LeAnn here at the restaurant?" I asked.

"Actually, we do. She was employee of the month in January. We keep the photos up for each employee for the entire year and then start over again." He stood. "The wall of photos is in the hallway. We don't have room for an entire year of pictures in the restaurant area."

"Can you point out LeAnn's?"

"Of course."

Devon and I followed David out of his office and

walked down the hallway that opened to the kitchen. He pointed at the first photo on the wall. "That's LeAnn."

I let out a long breath—the photo was a match to our victim. "Thank you, Mr. Conn. We appreciate your help, but there's one more thing."

"Sure, name it."

"Is LeAnn's husband listed as her emergency contact?"

"Probably, but let's go double-check. Did something happen to her? Is LeAnn okay?"

"I'm sorry, but we can't discuss her condition with anyone but her husband. I'm sure you understand."

His face wrinkled into a frown as he took a seat at his desk and tapped the computer keys. "Here we go. Yes, Mark Morrison is listed as her next of kin."

"And is there a phone number for him?"

"There is." David wrote it down and slid the piece of paper across his desk to me. "Will you inform me when you can?"

"We will, and thank you." Rue and I stood, shook his hand, and left the restaurant.

Back at the car, I dropped down into the driver's seat with a grunt. Rue mirrored my action in the passenger seat. "How do we call the husband, wherever he is, and tell him his wife is dead?" I asked.

Devon huffed. "You can bet he'll ask how she died."

I turned the key in the ignition and shifted into gear. "No matter what, we need to confirm it's her before we call him."

"But the employee-of-the-month photo pretty much confirmed it already," Rue said.

"I know. Let's go back to the scene and see what's up."

It was almost eleven o'clock by the time we returned

to the school. The forensic van was pulling out of the lot when we arrived. I lowered my window and flagged them down.

"What's the latest?" I asked as I slowed to a stop.

Martin was behind the wheel, so he did the talking. "Same as Valerie's. The intestines and pancreas are still inside her, but the heart, lungs, liver, and kidneys are gone. Seems like the same MO but just a different dump site. Maybe the killer got wind that Valerie was found in the marsh."

"Maybe. Find anything of evidentiary value?" I wiped my forehead while waiting for his answer. The temperature was a humid eighty-five degrees and climbing.

"Nothing worth noting on the ground and no tire marks around the car. We dusted the vehicle for prints and will check the database when we get back to the lab. Unfortunately, just a dead woman with her organs removed and a store receipt in her pocket. No phone and no wallet."

"Receipt? Could you read it, or was it ruined by the blood?"

"No. Luckily, it was in her back pocket. Tapper found it after they lifted her out of the car."

"Who has it now?"

"It's in an evidence bag in Royce's custody."

"Okay, thanks, guys. Talk later." I shifted into gear and continued to the back of the last building. Tapper and Terry were still on scene with the officers, Royce, Lawrence, and Bentley. I parked, and we headed their way.

"Find out anything?" Royce asked as we got closer.

"Yeah. Neighbor told us where LeAnn worked and said the husband was out of town."

"That probably explains why nobody has reported her missing," Lawrence said.

Rue nodded. "We figured the same."

"We went to her place of employment and spoke with the manager, and he showed us a picture of her." I tipped my head toward Tapper's van. "It matched the woman in the car. We got the husband's phone number but haven't made the call yet."

Royce groaned. "Telling a spouse news like that over the phone is the worst way to break it to someone."

I had to agree, but we didn't know when Mark was scheduled to come home. I was sure that after numerous calls to LeAnn's phone without an answer, he would start to worry anyway.

"It's your call, Boss. What do you want us to do?"

"Damn it. Where's her phone and purse? She had to have some money since there was a receipt dated from yesterday in her pocket."

"The killer likely took everything. Speaking of that receipt, it can give us a timeline of events."

"Right. Here's the picture I took with my phone. The original is already sealed in an evidence bag." Royce texted the copy to my phone. "Follow up with that, and I'll make the call to the husband."

"You sure?"

"Yep."

I pulled the slip of paper the restaurant manager had given me out of my pocket and handed it to Royce. "Do you want us to head out now, or do you need us here?"

"Go ahead. I'll have Bentley and Lawrence talk to LeAnn's neighbors even though I doubt that LeAnn or Valerie were actually targeted by someone they knew. I'd consider their murders crimes of opportunity instead."

Rue added his opinion. "It's looking more like that

now that two women have been killed. We'll check into the possibility of Valerie and LeAnn knowing each other, but a young single woman having a friendship with a fortysomething married woman is unlikely."

Royce grumbled. "Keep me posted on what you find out with that receipt."

"Will do." I stared at the receipt Royce had texted to my phone. It was from a coffee kiosk at the mall and time-stamped at two minutes after ten last night. "Looks like she grabbed a coffee to go. Let's see if anyone at the coffee stand knows her."

Chapter 18

Rue and I headed to the mall. Since we'd been right across the street just an hour earlier, it seemed like we were wasting precious time, but back then, we hadn't known about the receipt. We went to the customer service counter and asked where we could find Grind Time. We were told it was up the escalator and to the left and that we couldn't miss it. Once we reached the second floor, the colorful stand was thirty feet to our left. We approached the young lady sitting behind the counter, and she stood when we reached her.

"Hi, what can I get you?" she asked.

I looked at Rue and shrugged. "Two coffees, please, and some information."

She wrinkled her forehead as she prepared the coffee. "Information about what?"

"Do you know LeAnn Morrison?"

She laughed. "I don't know who you are. Why would I answer that?"

Rue moved his jacket aside, exposing his badge, then smiled. "Because we asked nicely."

She rolled her eyes. "Yeah, I know LeAnn. She works in that shoe store behind you, but I'm sure you know that."

We acted as though we did. "Of course, but she isn't at work today. Do you know her well?"

"Well enough. She buys coffee from me whenever I'm working."

"Do you work until the mall closes?"

"Nope. Only from three until six every day. It isn't a lot, but it pays for my gas and personal needs. I live with my folks and take college courses online." She stuck out her hand. "By the way, I'm Callie."

"Nice to meet you, Callie." I brought up the picture of the receipt. "This is from last night." I pointed at the initials. "Do you know who J. L. is?"

"Sure, that's Josh Lang. He takes over three nights a week when my shift ends. He shuts down the kiosk when the mall closes."

"So, he would have created this receipt for one caramel latte?"

"Yep. Probably the last sale of the night. Sounds like something LeAnn would have bought."

"Right, it was LeAnn's receipt."

Callie looked confused. "So why aren't you talking to LeAnn about whatever it is you're here for?"

I skirted her question and asked one of my own. "Did you see LeAnn yesterday?"

"Sure. She comes in during my shift. She says hi, starts work, and then buys a coffee at her six o'clock break. We usually talk during those ten minutes. After that, Josh takes over for me, LeAnn goes back to work, and I go home. Is something wrong? With LeAnn, I mean?"

I gave her my best smile and handed her my card.

"Nothing we can't handle. Appreciate your help, Callie, and call if anything comes to mind." I was happy that my new business cards showed me only as Detective Mitch Cannon, not listing the department I worked in. That would be a dead giveaway as to why we were asking about LeAnn.

We spoke briefly with the manager of the shoe store, and he confirmed that LeAnn had worked her entire shift last night and left when everyone else did. Nothing was out of the ordinary.

Rue and I headed downstairs to the customer service counter, where we asked for the location of the security office. We hoped to see LeAnn on camera as she left the building. That would tell us whether she was abducted right there in the mall's parking lot or somewhere off-site.

The woman behind the counter said we weren't allowed to go into the security office without an escort, but she would call somebody out to meet with us. We said that was fine.

Minutes later, an older man who looked like he could be a retired police officer walked out, introduced himself as Tim Hein, and escorted us back. We explained what we needed, and he said he was more than happy to help. We'd learned that he was indeed a retired cop who had moved south after putting in his twenty years of service at the Milwaukee Police Department.

I thought about how small our world actually was and asked if he was familiar with North Bend. He said yes, and I told him we'd worked a case last year with an FBI agent from North Bend.

Once we'd finished the courtesies and got down to business, we asked to see the footage of the shoppers and employees as they exited the building.

He scratched his head. "That's a tall order, Detectives. Our employees leave anywhere between ten and eleven p.m. If they're a manager, it's the latter. The mall has cameras that cover every exit, and we have twelve of them. Is there a way to narrow down your request?"

Rue took over. "Well, the employee was a part-time worker, so she wasn't a manager, and she worked at the shoe store on the second floor."

"There are three shoe stores upstairs. Do you know which one?"

"Yes, Barker Shoes."

"Good. That helps. The nearest exit to that side of the building is the northwest exit. The woman you're looking for probably went out that door."

"We have a coffee receipt of hers that was time-stamped two minutes after ten," I said.

"Okay, then that would put her downstairs and at the exit by six or seven minutes after the hour. Would you recognize her if you saw her? The cameras capture images in color, but you'd likely see her only from the back."

Since we'd never seen LeAnn alive, I had no idea if we'd recognize her, but we had seen the clothes she was found in that morning. My assumption was that they were the same clothes she'd worn during her shift last night. We would also watch for a woman carrying a coffee cup from Grind Time.

"So, is that the door you want me to bring up?"

I cocked my head at Rue and said yes. We had to start somewhere. "Start the footage right at ten o'clock, Tim."

"You got it."

I recalled the blouse LeAnn had on in the car. The front had turned a sickly black from all the blood, but the sleeves and collar were still green. Her pants were black anyway. We were looking for a woman wearing a green blouse, black pants, and likely carrying a purse and a coffee cup. She also had shoulder-length brown hair. I was confident that if she walked out that door, we would recognize her.

When Tim hit Play, I double-checked the time stamp. It was ten o'clock, and the date was correct. Within a few minutes, she might exit through that door.

My eyes were locked on the screen. Customers carrying bags were walking out, and the lot was clearing. I glanced at the time stamp again—10:02. LeAnn was upstairs paying for her coffee. How much time she still had among the living, we didn't know. Tapper had estimated that she'd been dead between eight and ten hours when he arrived at the scene. That meant she had been killed in the parking lot or abducted there and killed shortly afterward.

I sucked in a deep breath and focused on the screen. I pictured LeAnn taking the escalator down to the first floor and walking the hallway to the exit. If only we could turn back time.

"There!" Rue's shout startled me out of my vision. "That has to be her, but she isn't alone like we figured."

"Employees often walk out with other employees," Tim said. "Safety in numbers you know, especially at night."

We were aware of the saying, but in LeAnn's case, it didn't matter. She had been chosen by sick individuals, and her fate was in their hands. Why it was her and not the woman with her, we didn't know, but the footage might answer that question.

As we continued to watch, I asked Tim if he recognized the other woman.

He shrugged. "It's hard to say from behind, plus I don't know many of the store employees. There are two groups in Security—the mall walkers and the monitor watchers. I fit into the second group. That lady is either a friend of LeAnn's who was shopping until closing or an employee who shopped before her shift and had her purchases set aside until she left for the night."

Knowing who that woman was could be helpful, and we would get back to that later. For the moment, we needed to watch whatever played out in front of us. It was hard to see the women clearly as they walked farther out into the lot. Their images became fuzzy. I squinted and asked Tim to pause the video.

"Is there anything you can do to sharpen the footage?"

"Sorry but no. Night images are tough the way it is, and as people get farther from the camera, the worse it becomes."

I gave Tim a nod. We could only watch and hopefully be able to tell what was going on. The women veered slightly to the right and stopped at a car centered in the lot. I couldn't tell the make or model, but it wasn't LeAnn's car. The trunk opened and closed, then a minute later, the car drove away. We saw someone we presumed to be LeAnn continue walking until we couldn't see her any longer. I checked the time—10:14.

We waited. She must have driven there from home, and sooner or later, we would see headlights or taillights pull away—if the camera reached that far.

I turned to Tim. "Are there cameras farther out in the lot or just what's on the storefronts?"

"Only what's attached to the building. Honestly, we've never had anyone question how far the cameras pick up images or if the range goes as far as the outer lots. I'd have to make a call to the company who sold the cameras to us and installed them."

"How long would it take to get that information?"

Tim shrugged. "I should know by this afternoon."

"Okay, good. We'll watch for another few minutes. Maybe we'll see a car go past on the frontage road."

It was nearing ten thirty on the screen when two vehicles exited out the main entrance. Tim had switched cameras so we could see the frontage road, which went from the outer lots to the street that turned in at the mall.

"Did you see that?" Rue asked. "Two vehicles just left, one right after the other."

"Right, but we didn't see where they came from. It could still be employees leaving out of different areas of the parking lot."

"I couldn't tell what the vehicles were, but I could see that one was a light color and large."

Rue's comment made me think. Jacob Kenney had a large white van. Could it be him after all? I asked Tim to back up the footage a smidge, then I took a picture of the vehicles. I didn't know whether Tech could sharpen that picture, but I would urge them to try.

I gave Tim my card, asked him to call as soon as he knew about the cameras, then we left. I needed to get that photo in Tech's capable hands as soon as I could.

I told Rue my thoughts as I drove to the precinct. "Do you think that large light-colored vehicle could be a van, as in a white Econoline van?"

He frowned. "As in a Jacob Kenney kind of van?"

"Maybe."

"Then how did LeAnn's car get to the school? A second person helping out? Somebody who knows Jacob by name, like Dylan Marx?"

"That's also a maybe. I sure as hell hope that Tech can give us more." I grinned at Rue. "And they haven't let us down yet."

Chapter 19

Rue updated Royce as I drove to the precinct. According to Royce, he would be heading back soon. Tapper had left with LeAnn's remains, and the husband had been called. He was on his way back to Savannah from Cleveland, and nothing had been found around the car that could point a finger at anyone.

That school had been shut down for twenty years, ever since a larger high school was built. It had no electricity, let alone cameras, and the immediate area around the school was mostly vacant lots littered with trash.

The crime lab's flatbed had taken the car to the evidence garage, and the yellow tape had been taken down. The average passerby would have no idea what had taken place there earlier.

We arrived at the precinct and stopped at our tech department before going upstairs. Tom and Dan gave us their full attention as I explained what we needed. I asked if it was even possible to enhance the photo I'd taken from the video.

Tom had me email the photo to him. Dropping the

image into their software program was the only way to try, he said, but he couldn't guarantee a better outcome than what we already had.

"Night videos are grainy to say the least, but we'll do what we can with what we have to work with. The actual video would be better," Tom said.

"And that may be a possibility, but let's see what you can do to enhance it first. I'm thinking it could be an extended white van, but that's just my wishful thinking talking out loud. I'm not trying to sway you in any direction."

Tom chuckled. "We'll get back to you with our best results before the end of the shift."

With a nod, I thanked them, and Devon and I headed upstairs.

We grabbed sandwiches from the vending machine as we passed the lunchroom. I wanted to make sure we didn't miss the call from Tim, the mall's security guard. If the cameras didn't reach the spot where LeAnn had parked, then we would never know the when, how, or who of the abduction. I was counting on Tech to give us something. The vehicle behind the one in question could be LeAnn's car. Learning whether she or someone else was driving it and whether that person could be identified might break open the case. There were a lot of "ifs" involved and, so far, not a lot of "absolutes" about anything other than the fact that two women were murdered, and their organs had been removed.

I devoured my two egg salad sandwiches and washed them down with a cola. A package of chocolate chip cookies would be my dessert. It would hold me over until that night when I enjoyed whatever Marie or Mom prepared for supper. I glanced over at Rue, and his sandwiches were eaten as well. He was working on the first of two bags of potato chips, and cookies would finish up his meal.

I wiped my mouth just as my phone rang. After a quick gulp of cola, I answered. "Detective Cannon speaking."

"Detective, it's Tim Hein. I learned more about the mall's security cameras."

"Great. What were you told?"

"Probably not the news you were hoping to hear."

My optimism vanished as quickly as his words. "Okay, let's hear it."

"The range of clarity between the building to the point of something becoming unidentifiable is about three hundred feet."

"Slightly less than the size of a football field."

"That's correct. Anything the cameras catch beyond that will be a blur."

"Then why didn't we see LeAnn reach her car at all?"

"I'm guessing the angle of that camera had a lot to do with it. My guess is that it, or maybe even all of them, points somewhat down instead of in a straight line facing out. It's probably a deliberate act so the cameras can record activity from the exits out into the main areas of the lot. Honestly, except at peak holiday times, those outer lots don't get much use."

I thought about LeAnn's car, a late model Corolla. Could she have parked away from other cars just so her doors wouldn't get dinged? It was a possibility and likely a deadly mistake. "I have just one more question."

"Sure, go ahead."

"Do any of the cameras point directly at the main entrance with the street, and if they do, which is the closest one?"

"There's a camera at the entryway that points at the mall's backlit marquee. We've had vandalism there in the past with people breaking the signage, so management had a camera installed on the stone façade that reads Southgate Mall. That stone wall faces the marquee."

"And would it capture the vehicles coming into and out of the mall's frontage road?"

"Yes. That wouldn't be a problem."

"Even at night?"

"Even at night. It's higher than eye level, of course, because the marquee is elevated."

"Is that camera activated at all times too?"

"It is."

"And one more question."

"Go ahead."

"Can you segregate the times for its playback, and can you email that timeframe to me?"

"I'll ask our supervisor. He's more technical than I am. What times are you interested in?"

"Last night from nine thirty to eleven thirty."

"Okay, I'll get back to you as soon as I can."

I thanked Tim again and hung up. If our tech department couldn't get a clear image of those two vehicles driving down the frontage road several hundred feet from the building's camera, then maybe the camera at the entryway could. It was worth checking out.

Chapter 20

Teddy slid the tote out of the closet, lifted the lid, moved the clothes aside, and stared at the cash. He wanted to make sure it was safe.

"Whatcha doing, brother?"

"Worrying."

"About what?"

Teddy pointed his chin at the tote. "About that money. We have several hundred thousand dollars here that's lying unprotected in a twenty-dollar plastic bin."

Chase laughed. "Would you feel better if I placed a gun inside?" He took a seat at the foot of the bed and stared into the tote. "Man, if that isn't a kickass sight, then I don't know what is." He grinned at Teddy. "Lighten up, bro. Nobody knows that there's money under our dirty clothes, and besides that, nobody knows what we're doing."

"What if someone broke in?"

"I'd be here even if you were at work. Speaking of that, when are you going to quit that shitty job?"

"As soon as I know we've gotten away with this. If we ever piss off your contacts, they may rat us out."

"And then we'll rat them out too. That's the beauty of everyone having something to lose. Nobody wants to lose the free-flowing money, so they keep their mouths shut. No bragging to friends, no pillow talk with women, no drunken diarrhea of the mouth. Not a word to anyone and we'll be golden. Hear me?"

"Yeah, but I still think the money should be in a safe deposit box."

"I'll think about it, but all that does is leave a paper trail. Not the smartest idea, Teddy."

"Then something else. How about a safe in the house? A big one that can't be carried out. We'll bolt it to the floor. That would work."

Chase agreed. He needed to keep his brother cool-headed. "Yeah, that would work just fine, and we can afford it. We'll buy one. I promise."

"Okay, but let's do it now. I'm working later, and I'd like to have that safe in the house and set up before I go to work."

"No sweat."

The brothers headed to the nearest gun supply store. Nobody would question them for buying a large, heavy gun safe. But theirs wouldn't contain more than two pistols, guns that were passed down from their grandfather and that they'd had for years.

It was nearly six o'clock by the time they found a safe that would fit into the master bedroom walk-in closet, a safe they could actually maneuver into the house without additional help. The safe had a digital pad and backup key entry. It was perfect.

Once the brothers had moved the hanging clothes to

the opposite side of the closet and manhandled the safe into place, they decided on a four-digit code, and each had his own key as a backup to open it. They stacked the banded cash onto the shelves, stood back, and stared in admiration.

"Now that's a pretty sight," Teddy said, "and a *safe* one." He laughed at his own way with words. "I feel better already."

Chase patted his brother's shoulder. "Sometimes you come up with really good ideas, bro, and this was one of them." He joined in on the word play. "Better *safe* than sorry. Now let's hang those clothes back where they were. Nobody will ever know the safe is there."

Minutes later, Teddy looked at his watch. "We finished just in time. Now I've got to get to work. Want to drop me off or just hang out here?"

Chase swatted the air. "I'm good. Go ahead, and don't work too hard."

Chapter 21

I glanced at the time on my phone—I was becoming anxious. "Damn it. What's taking Tom so long to get back to us?"

Rue shook his head and stared at the enhanced image Tech had given us of that still shot I'd taken. "I hate to say this, but that picture, even though it's obviously a van, isn't going to get us a warrant. No judge in the county will pony up a warrant based on an image of a blurry van that resembles the white van Jacob Kenney owns. Not just because he used to abuse animals. He hasn't been on anyone's radar since he got out of jail."

"So how can we build a case against him if we can't search his premises or vehicle?"

Rue shrugged. "Good question. The only way is if Tim from the mall can get us a clear look at that van as it turns onto the street. Maybe we can catch the rear plate or see who is behind the wheel. Or maybe we'll see the Econoline badge on the rear panel. Something has to work. We need to dig deeper into Jacob and Dylan Marx. My gut says they're both lying to us."

I cracked my neck, and Rue groaned.

"Dude, you're going to mess up a vertebra doing that."

"Nah, it relieves the tension I'm feeling." I let out a long-winded sigh. "Royce will send us packing as soon as he realizes we're still here. I was sure by now, Tim would have called."

When we heard footsteps heading our way, we stared at the door.

"Great, it's probably Royce. You jinxed us by saying his name."

"Whose name?"

I raised a brow and grinned at Royce standing in the doorway. "Guess you heard that, huh?"

"Some of it, and why are you two still here? I thought you left a half hour ago."

"That was the plan, but I guess we're waiting on a phone call," Devon said.

"From?" Royce asked.

I took over. "Tim at the mall. There was the chance of getting a better look at those two vehicles we saw video of."

"Did you give him your card?"

"Yep."

"Then he can call your cell if he actually has something for you. We're on a tight budget now, and the head honchos haven't actually approved overtime yet, so hit the road."

I pushed back my chair and stretched. "Roger that, Boss. We're heading out now."

Rue and I parted ways in the lot, and as I drove home, my instincts told me that Tim was having problems. If everything was good to go with that camera footage at the mall entrance, we would have heard back from him hours ago. Something wasn't right. I didn't have his cell number, and it was doubtful that a mall security office would give it to me on request. Everyone had a right to privacy, so I would have to wait.

Once at the house, I checked my phone every fifteen minutes as I played board games with the girls. Supper was almost ready, and it was unlikely I would hear from Tim at all that night. Later, after we'd eaten, I slipped away and contacted the precinct to see if Tim had called there looking for me. He hadn't.

After saying good night to the family, I headed upstairs to bed. Sleep didn't come easily. I kept thinking about Jacob. I was sure that van belonged to him, yet why would he risk abducting women in public places just to kill and remove their organs? It didn't make sense. Everyone's life had value, but if he wanted to kill someone that badly, there were other options where the likelihood of being caught on camera wasn't as high. Maybe the thrill of being caught was as much of an adrenaline rush to him as the kill itself.

Did he sacrifice their organs during a ceremony then ask for forgiveness during that very ritual only to repeat it again? Is he addicted to these heinous crimes, or does Dylan have influence over him?

I didn't have those answers. I didn't even know if I was on the right track, but without some actions resulting in their arrests, I had no idea of the men's personalities or level of risk-taking.

The last thing I remembered before falling asleep was rolling over, punching my pillow, and checking the time—three a.m. I was pretty certain I would be living on caffeine the next day.

Chapter 22

"Wow, you look like hell."

I flipped Rue the bird. "Thanks. I feel like hell, too, since I literally got four hours of sleep."

He chuckled. "That isn't the first time you went with hardly any sleep. You must be getting old."

I flipped him two birds and plopped down at my desk. I leaned back in my chair and closed my eyes.

"Don't do that for too long. You'll be snoring before you know it."

"How do you do it, Rue?"

"Do what?"

"Sleep at night instead of lying awake thinking about the case."

"I compartmentalize."

I snickered. "I'm serious."

"So am I. I drink a couple of beers while I watch the news, then I give myself a half hour to review the case in my mind. I write down things that I may have to discuss with you or the group the next day. That cleans my slate, so to speak. After that, I down a melatonin tablet, hit the hay, and sleep like a baby."

I groaned. "That saying is ridiculous. Babies don't sleep worth a shit."

"Says the bachelor."

"I have two sisters who loved to complain about the lack of sleep they got when the kids were babies."

Devon laughed. "Guess you didn't fall far from the sibling tree."

I shook my head. "Touché."

"So, nothing from Tim Hein?"

"Nope. I'll give him an hour or so, then I'll call the security office myself."

"Well, briefing is in ten. I'd suggest you grab a coffee so you don't sleep through it."

"Yeah, that's not a bad idea."

We headed down the hallway and bought our coffees. After taking a few sips to make more room in my cup, I bought an espresso, too, and poured it into my coffee.

Rue grinned. "You good?"

"I should be, but elbow me if I start nodding off."

"Will do. Come on. Let's head down."

By the time we settled into our seats, the briefing was about to begin. Since Royce hadn't pulled us aside to tell us anything urgent when we arrived that morning, I figured the meeting would be brief and uneventful. I was right. No murders were committed overnight, or at least no bodies were discovered yet, and that was a plus. Our day was starting in a somewhat normal manner. Royce mentioned the possibility of having a local FBI profiler go over the police reports we'd put together on Valerie and LeAnn's murders to see if they could shed some light on who we were looking for. Short of sitting on Jacob's house, which wasn't yet warranted, we had no suspects or hard leads. We didn't even have anything to air on the news. My only hope for moving the case along was to get something from that camera at the mall entrance.

I was anxious to get to my office and couldn't wait for the meeting to end. It concluded in under fifteen minutes, and thankfully, there weren't many questions. Other than the profiler suggestion, Royce had mentioned something about starting over and interviewing everyone again, beginning with the people Valerie knew. I was barely listening. I just wanted to speak with Tim Hein. If that camera couldn't help us, we truly would be starting from scratch.

By 8:50, I was seated at my desk, and the light on my phone wasn't flashing—no messages.

"Mitch, just call him. You're going to drive yourself nuts if you don't find out what that camera does or doesn't show."

"Yeah, you're right. Enough waiting." I woke up my laptop, found the 800 number for the mall, and dialed it. I imagined it would take me to an answering service, which would then transfer me to the department I needed.

"Southgate Mall."

"Hello, I need to be connected to the security department."

"I'm sorry, sir, but the mall doesn't open until nine o'clock. The only businesses that are open are the ones with outdoor access like restaurants."

I hung up and grumbled with seven more minutes to wait. I left my desk and went to the lunchroom. I needed another coffee to go with the aspirin I was about to take. Stress and lack of sleep were giving me a headache.

After I returned to my desk and sat down, I tried the

call again and was immediately connected to the security department. I sighed in relief.

"Getting through?"

I gave Rue a thumbs-up. "Yep. Now to find out why Tim didn't call back yesterday."

The call was answered by a man whose voice didn't sound familiar. I told him who I was and asked for Tim.

"Sorry, Detective Cannon, but Tim had to leave town. His wife was involved in a car accident while visiting family in Wisconsin."

"Oh no. Will she be okay?"

"We haven't heard from him yet, so I couldn't say, but I sure hope so. They've been married for over twenty years. Is there something I can help you with?"

"Yes. I was working with Tim yesterday on parking lot footage from the night before. What we had didn't extend to the outer lots, so he suggested looking at the mall marquee camera to see if any questionable vehicles passed by. Tim was going to check with the supervisor to see if the time in question could be segregated from the rest of the footage and emailed to me."

"I'm the supervisor, Larry Grant, and Tim never mentioned it, but he was pretty shaken up as soon as he learned about Janet's accident."

"And rightfully so. I completely understand. I thought there was a problem with the footage or possibly that the camera didn't catch anything worthwhile."

"Well, I'll take a look myself, and yes, I can pull out a certain part of the recording. Got a time in mind?"

"I do. From nine thirty to eleven thirty night before last."

"Okay, I need your email address, and I'll send it right over."

I was relieved that I would finally have that camera

footage in front of me. I needed it to prove that the van in the grainy image from the frontage road footage was Jacob's van. At least then, the likelihood of getting a warrant would go up exponentially. I thanked Larry and hung up.

"The supervisor is emailing the footage to me in a few minutes. We need something off that van that can substantiate my theory of it being Jacob's."

Rue shook his head. "Don't become overly confident. That's usually when the letdowns happen."

"Yeah, yeah. We'll see." I waited on pins and needles. I was sure it would take at least a half hour before the video attachment arrived in my in-box. "Hand me that picture Tech enhanced."

Rue handed it across our desks. "What are you looking for?"

"Something, anything, that could match up with Jacob's van."

"We don't even have a picture of his van. We only know that it's an Econoline, and if we don't catch that badge on the new footage, it's not going to help us at all."

I rubbed my eyes. "You do have a point. Maybe after we review the video that faces the mall marquee sign, we should take a trip out to Jacob's place again and discreetly snap off a few pictures. The parking lot is a public area."

Rue chuckled. "Now you're splitting hairs. It's part of the apartment complex property."

I waved off his comment. "I'll be careful. Nobody will even know I'm taking pictures. If I have to, I'll take pictures from the sidewalk."

"First things first. Let's look at the footage."

I glanced at my emails, and a new one had just come

in. "Here we go. Scoot on over, and let's see what we've got." I waited as Rue wheeled his chair to the side of my desk. "Are you ready?"

He nodded. "Whenever you are."

Larry's email had come in with the video. He confirmed the time and date I'd asked for. "Looks like everything is a go." I clicked on the full-screen icon then hit Play. We were staring at the backlit marquee, which showed the store names on that side of the mall. I focused on the video, and the street began to lighten up. I pointed at the screen. "That has to be from headlights coming toward the exit. Any minute now." I leaned in closer. We would watch it in real time then in slow motion. I was sure that over the next few minutes, we'd back it up a dozen times. A white blur sped past the camera, and another blur came right behind it.

"Wait a minute. What the hell was that?" Rue asked.

"Those two vehicles, but I had no idea the camera was mounted that close to the driveway. It's literally ten feet from the vehicles. How are we going to see the entire size and shape of that van or even know if the other car is LeAnn's?" My disappointment was contagious.

Devon groaned. "Back it up and go ahead in slow motion. Maybe slowing down the footage will show us something. Plus, all we're seeing is the top third of the van."

"Tim did say the camera sat above eye level."

Rue huffed. "It's got to be damn near the top of the sign, meaning we'll catch the drivers' foreheads at the most."

My hopes for that video helping us were gone. I backed up the footage, watched it at a half-dozen speeds, and even took screen shots. All I got was a close-up of a big blurry vehicle passing by.

"Even if we did take pictures of Jacob's van, it isn't going to help. We can't make out shit from the camera to compare anything to," Rue said.

"We could put a tracking device under Jacob's van," I said.

Devon laughed. "Tell me that was a joke."

I grumbled. "Yeah, legally, it's a joke, but if I had any say in it—"

"But you don't." Rue rolled his eyes. "Do you think Royce is really going to have a profiler come in?"

I shrugged. "Sounds like a waste of time and money to me. We don't even have a type of person for them to profile. They take unnecessary risks. There. I just profiled the person or people involved, and it took two seconds."

"Has anyone looked up how many 2011 white Econoline vans are in the city?"

"I don't think so, but we can get on that ourselves." I tapped my pen against the desk.

Rue grinned. "Looks like something is percolating in your mind."

"It is, but we'll have to do it after dark."

Chapter 23

I hated to report our findings to Royce, but we needed to come up with a different approach. I also wanted to tell him my new idea, and it didn't have anything to do with a profiler. I planned to give him my opinion of that tactic, too, although as our sergeant, he could do anything he wanted to further the investigation.

Rue and I went together. Courage and strength in numbers, I always said. I gave Royce's door a light rap since it was partially open.

"Come in, guys." He pointed his chin at the chairs, and we sat.

"Just wanted to let you know the mall videos didn't help. We really don't even know if those two vehicles would be helpful. We didn't see LeAnn walk to either of them since she was out of camera range before she climbed into a vehicle."

Royce grunted. "Night images and videos are terrible to begin with."

"That too," Rue said.

Royce stared at the printed sheet in my hand. "Whatcha got there?"

"It's the image of the white van that Tech enhanced for us. Honestly, it isn't much better, maybe twenty percent at most."

The sergeant shook his head. "Can't make a case with that. If it had an identifiable feature to compare to Jacob's vehicle, then maybe."

I cleared my throat. "Well…"

Royce's eyebrows shot up. "Speak up, Cannon."

"We know the distance that image is from the camera, and it is during the night. I was thinking we can see if Jacob's van is in the parking lot of his apartment, get about the same distance away from it, and take some pictures at night."

"You think a cell phone photo is going to compare to an image from a high-quality surveillance camera?"

"The camera quality can't be that great if you can't make out shit from a hundred yards away, sir." I made sure to add "sir" so it didn't sound like I was being disrespectful.

Royce scratched his chin. "Doesn't mean he's going to be home."

"Then we'll wait," Rue added.

I appreciated his support since that was the first time he'd heard my suggestion.

"On your own time?" Royce asked. "You know overtime hasn't been approved."

"We know." I jokingly added my earlier comment to Rue about using a tracker, and Royce chuckled. "If only the law allowed that without just cause, but it doesn't, so don't get any ideas."

"We won't, Boss."

"Okay, anything else?"

"About that profiler."

"Yes, what about him?"

"We already know the killer is brazen and slippery. We know they aren't afraid of taking risks. We know they're one of two types of people—the kind who use organs in ceremonies or the kind who use them to make money. What more can an FBI profiler tell us that we don't already know?"

Royce nodded. It was possible he was seeing my point.

"I'll give you three days to come up with a real lead or the profiler gets a call."

There was nothing I could do but thank him. We would get with Lawrence and Bentley and see if they had any more ideas or information to share. After that, Rue and I would head to Jacob Kenney's apartment.

Lawrence and Bentley told us they hadn't learned anything new from speaking with LeAnn's neighbors. Bentley added that they'd asked the neighbors if LeAnn had ever mentioned the name Valerie Dawson. According to Bentley, that name didn't sound familiar to any of them.

I updated the guys on the fact that LeAnn's husband was coming in first thing tomorrow to have a sit-down with Royce and the rest of us before identifying LeAnn's remains.

"Does he know…"

I looked at Lawrence. "That her organs had been removed?"

"Yeah."

I grimaced. "I'm not quite sure how much Royce told him over the phone. We'll probably learn more at that meeting in the morning. I'd suggest we keep quiet and only talk when we're directly asked questions. Royce will likely lead the conversation anyway."

It was time to call it a day. Rue and I said good night and reminded the guys about overtime. "Royce will tear you a new one if you two don't leave soon. Tomorrow is another day, and maybe we'll get new leads after hearing what LeAnn's husband has to say."

Rue and I grabbed supper at Rose's Cantina, and once darkness took over the sky, we headed to Jacob's apartment complex.

When we arrived, I drove slowly along the parking lot then spotted the van. I pointed through my window. "There it is. Dead center in the lot. How the hell am I going to get a picture of it with vehicles all around it?"

Devon shrugged.

"When we saw it the first time, it was in the spot nearest the street. I assumed that was his assigned space, but seeing where it's parked now tells me a different story."

"We'll have to do the best we can," Rue said. "There's no other choice."

I parked my rental and planned to drop off Rue at the precinct to pick up his vehicle once we were done for the night. Luckily, we wouldn't have to wait for Jacob to come home from who knew where.

We exited the car and backed up to an area we guessed was about a hundred feet out, then I pointed my phone's camera at the lot. Irritated, I shook my head.

"This isn't a good spot. I can't even see the van. Let's cross the street and try it from a different angle."

"No matter what, we aren't going to get a full side view of it unless we try some other time when the van is out in the open. That would require following him, and if I'm not mistaken, we don't have permission to work overtime. Royce sure as hell won't let us follow Jacob around the city during work hours, plus that would defeat the point anyway. It would be broad daylight outside."

I grumbled. "Come on."

"Where?"

"To get up close and personal with that van. Maybe there's something else besides the length and shape we can use to compare the vans."

I looked both ways then stepped off the curb, crossed the street, and entered the parking lot. As crowded as the lot was, nobody would notice us weaving in and out between cars.

We reached Jacob's van, where I snapped pictures of all four sides. The vehicles were parked so close to each other I couldn't even get a full-length picture of the van from either side. We looked for window stickers, scratches, dents, or anything that would set the van apart. It was relatively clean and devoid of stickers. If anything was going to help us, it would have to be something large enough to stand out in that video of the white blur zooming past the camera.

"Hey!"

I rounded the van to the driver's side, where Rue stood. "What's up?"

"Notice anything?" He grinned. "Or the lack of?"

I stared at the van, then it hit me like a ton of bricks. I looked through the windshield and confirmed that there was a mirror on the passenger's side.

"I'll be damned. The driver's-side mirror is gone." I moved in closer and saw where the bolts had once been. "It must have been knocked off at some point and he never replaced it." I walked to the passenger side and snapped several pictures of the mirror. Luckily, the black trim stood out against the white van and would easily be noticeable on video—if the mirror was there. "Either that van speeding by the camera was Jacob's, or it wasn't, and the lack of a mirror on this van will give us that answer."

We left before somebody saw us and reported us to the police, which would be ironic. I dropped Rue off at his car, and tomorrow, we would compare the video to the pictures I took with my cell phone. It would be hard to wait, but we were off the clock, and I couldn't change that. One thing I did know was that morning couldn't come soon enough.

Chapter 24

After a long night of tossing and turning, I cracked one eye open and saw light coming through the blinds. Morning was finally here. I couldn't remember the last time I'd wanted daylight to arrive so badly. I climbed out of bed and hit the shower. Even though I hadn't caught up on my sleep yet, today was too important, and taking a second look at that video was all I could think about.

After a bowl of oatmeal, two coffees, and a slice of toast, I said goodbye to the family and left. I planned to arrive at the precinct earlier than usual, and as much as I wanted to queue up that video and watch it, I wouldn't do that until Rue arrived. It wouldn't be right, and partners always did right by each other.

Instead, I updated Royce on what Devon and I had discovered at Jacob's van last night. I went through the story with him about how the van was blocked in by other vehicles, so we'd decided to take a closer look. That was when Rue discovered the missing side mirror. That mirror, or lack of one, would tell us whether we were looking at Jacob's van or not.

After speaking with Royce, I returned to my office. I wanted everything ready to go as soon as Devon walked in. The best-case scenario would be to announce our results at that morning's briefing, and I couldn't wait.

Everything was set, and I waited on Rue to walk through the door. Finally, I heard footsteps coming down the hallway, and he crossed over the threshold.

"It's about time! Damn it, dude, how do you stay so calm and collected?"

Rue chuckled. "I can get all riled up like you, but that won't affect the outcome. It's going to be what it's going to be no matter how jacked up you get."

He had a point, but I didn't care. "Get your ass over here, and let's look at the footage again. I want something worthwhile to tell the group at the briefing."

Rue grabbed a guest chair and slid it over to my desk. He sat down and nodded. "Let 'er rip."

Since everything was ready to go, I hit Play, and we watched. Again, headlights brightened up the exit lane as they closed in on the camera. We would see the van in a second or two.

"Here we go." The white blur barreled past the camera as my finger hovered over Pause. I hit it then had to back it up slowly. "Wait a minute!" I couldn't believe what I was looking at. I hit Play again and backed it up as if the mirror would disappear, but it didn't. The van that whizzed past the camera had a perfectly good functioning driver's-side mirror. Seeing the black mirror trim told me my eyes weren't playing tricks on me—the vehicle wasn't Jacob's. I pounded the desk with my fist. "Are you seeing what I'm seeing?" My question was rhetorical, but Rue answered anyway.

"Yeah, damn it. I see the mirror too. That isn't Jacob's van, and it's time for our morning meeting."

"Shit. I guess there's no sense in sugarcoating anything. We tried to make a connection, it didn't work, and now we'll likely be starting from scratch."

I had to suck it up and accept the outcome. Maybe that white van had nothing to do with LeAnn's abduction at all. If that was the case, then learning how she and her car had gotten to the abandoned school would remain a mystery until something broke in the investigation.

I was thankful our meeting would be brief. We were scheduled to meet with LeAnn's husband in less than an hour. I had no idea what would be discussed other than the typical questions we asked any spouse of a murdered loved one. That time, however, the questioning would be in the conference room upstairs rather than in Mark Morrison's house.

After the morning updates, it was my turn to talk. Royce waved me over to the podium, likely expecting to hear promising news.

"Mitch, you want to share your findings?"

He clearly noticed my grimace when I stood, then his shoulders slumped. I wanted to say no and return to my seat, but I was already walking toward him and had to share the news no matter how disappointing. Only Bentley, Lawrence, and Royce knew where Rue and I had been going after we left the precinct last night, but I was about to reveal everything. I pulled in a deep breath and began.

After paraphrasing why we went to Jacob's house and my gut instincts about him, I said it turned out that I was wrong. As much as I'd wanted those vans to be one and the same, they weren't, and we were no further ahead in the investigation than we were when Valerie was found dead in the marsh. I explained that with help throughout the day, we would look up and investigate the owners of all white vans in the county. I hoped there weren't many, but I also explained that my idea of a white van being involved at all might be completely off target. I ended my portion of the meeting and returned to my seat.

Royce thanked Rue and me for the effort and said it was nearing the time to meet with LeAnn's husband. There was a chance that we might get more to work with from Mark Morrison himself.

The meeting was adjourned, and the room emptied. I was disappointed, but the job of finding and arresting the killer or killers wasn't mine alone, yet from the weight on my shoulders, it felt like it was.

We made a quick stop at our office to grab paper and pens in case Mr. Morrison had information that could help the investigation. While Royce talked to him, I would jot down questions I wanted to ask him myself.

With a carafe of hot coffee and Styrofoam cups in front of us, thanks to Diane at the front counter, we took our seats and waited. Diane said she would call the conference room as soon as Mark arrived. I took that time to write down a few questions I planned to ask if Royce didn't bring them up himself.

During our wait, Rue texted the crime lab to ask if they had finished going through LeAnn's car in case Mr. Morrison asked about it. I wasn't sure if Mark wanted the vehicle, but I doubted that seeing all the blood inside would help him with the agony he was likely going through.

According to Devon, Billy said they were still testing blood samples found throughout the car. He also said the interior of the car had been removed because of those tests. Stripping the interior out of that vehicle was definitely the smart thing to do.

Minutes later, Lawrence and Bentley entered the room and sat down. Royce, with a recorder in hand, walked in right after them. Since Mark wasn't a suspect in LeAnn's death and his alibi was solid, we weren't going to interview him in an interrogation room. The recorder would serve its purpose just fine.

The paper and pens seemed redundant, but still, I would have my questions in front of me when the time was right.

Royce tipped his wrist, checked the time, and settled in. "Sorry about the van situation, guys. It would have been a slam dunk if you were right."

I grumbled about how you can't win them all then asked Royce if we were going back to the beginning of the investigation with Valerie's murder.

"Let's see if Mark can shed any light. We'll discuss our options after he leaves."

Seconds later, the conference room phone rang. Royce nodded. "Guess he's here." He answered, told Diane to show Mark upstairs, then ended the call.

I asked Royce whether Mark knew how LeAnn was killed.

"Nope, and it won't do an ounce of good to tell him either."

The door opened, and Diane showed Mark in then left. We stood and introduced ourselves, and Royce offered Mark the chair next to him.

"First and foremost, the Savannah PD wants to offer you our deepest condolences," Royce said.

Mark cleared his throat. "Thank you. It's been a tough twenty-four hours."

Mark's eyes were red and swollen, a sight I'd seen far too many times in my years as a homicide detective.

Sarge continued. "We're hoping there might be something you can tell us that'll help move our investigation along. To be completely transparent with you, at this point, we have no suspects or even a motive for LeAnn's murder. We know LeAnn went to her jobs the day before yesterday, and my detectives here watched the mall video of LeAnn and another woman exiting the building together when the mall closed. It was confirmed that LeAnn worked her entire shift, bought a coffee at the kiosk just outside the shoe store, and then was seen leaving the building with an unknown woman. Could that woman be someone LeAnn had mentioned before? We'd like to interview her."

Mark sucked in a deep breath. "It was probably Margo. She's a friend of LeAnn's who works the night shift, too, at a clothing store on the first floor. Margo normally waits for LeAnn, then they leave the building together."

"Do you know Margo's last name and which store she works at?" Royce asked.

"Um"—Mark rubbed his forehead—"I think it's Dorfman, and she works at Just Jeans."

I wrote down the names and would call Margo later.

Royce continued. "What is your job, Mr. Morrison, and how often are you away from home?"

"I'm an accountant, and our company does business with big corporations from Ohio down to Miami. I happened to be in Cleveland when I got the call from you about LeAnn."

"Right. How long were you and LeAnn married, Mark?"

"Fifteen years. We chose not to have kids a long time

ago. We worked hard and wanted to retire in our early fifties." He smiled as tears ran down his cheeks. "We were going to travel the world."

"So your marriage was good? No problems or wandering eyes?"

"Our marriage was solid, Sergeant Royce. We were happy and content."

Royce looked at each of us. I took that as my cue to speak up.

"Sir, had LeAnn ever mentioned a customer bothering her, maybe an altercation at the pancake house or the shoe store?"

He shook his head. "Never anything that seemed to frighten her. She'd say something now and then about disgruntled customers, but nothing was ever aimed directly at her."

"Got it, and no disputes with neighbors?"

"No. Our neighbors are great." Mark wiped his eyes with the back of his hand. "This was a random act, wasn't it?"

Rue took over. "We believe so. The mall cameras showed the ladies walking to Margo's car, and then LeAnn continued on to the outer lot. The camera didn't pick up anything after that."

"I told her a million times not to park out there. It's too far from other cars when the mall closes and everyone leaves. She was adamant about avoiding door dingers on that car since it was new. She was so proud of it, and now—now it doesn't matter one damn bit."

"And we can discuss you taking possession of her car after the crime lab is done with it," Royce said. "Do you have any questions for us, Mark?"

"Yeah, when are you going to find her killer?"

Chapter 25

Once we returned to our office, I wasted no time making that call to Margo Dorfman. She hadn't heard about LeAnn's death since we'd needed that face-to-face with Mark before anything about LeAnn was released to the public.

Margo sounded shocked yet said she hadn't noticed a single thing unusual that night, and she hadn't seen anyone following them out of the building. She drove off like she did every night after she and LeAnn parted ways.

"I can't believe how stupid I am," she cried out through the phone.

"How so, ma'am?"

"There's no reason on earth I couldn't have driven LeAnn to her car each and every night we walked out together. She always parked so far out for fear of getting her new car dented by somebody's door."

"In your defense, Margo, how could you have known what would happen? It sounds like you had the same routine every night, and nothing bad happened before."

"I know but—"

"But you can't blame yourself. Blame the person who took her life. Tell me this. Did LeAnn always park in the same spot, and can you meet me there?"

"Yes, she parked within one or two spaces if another car happened to be in her usual one, and of course I'll meet you there. I don't work until two o'clock, so I can meet you around one thirty and show you her parking spot."

I sighed with relief. Maybe we would find a clue there. "That would really be helpful. You'll see my partner and me standing next to a black cruiser. Appreciate your help, Margo."

"Detective Cannon?"

"Yes, ma'am?"

"How is Mark holding up? He and LeAnn were a match made in heaven according to the way she always gushed about him."

"He's in rough shape now, but the PD will do whatever we can to help him get through this tough time, and we'll apprehend LeAnn's killer."

"Thank you, Detective Cannon, and I'll see you at one thirty. I need some time to process this horrible news."

I ended the call. It was time to get busy. We needed to check out the white vans in the county, and if nothing panned out, I would stop pursuing that angle, and the investigation would start over.

From my online research, it looked like there could be as many as two hundred white vans in Chatham County, a larger number than I wanted to see, but the information wasn't necessarily up to date. Hopefully, the DMV could help us with a current list of registered white vans in the county. After that, we'd take it from there. It was worth a shot to find out. I made the call, and after some hemming and hawing, they agreed to provide that list, although they said they couldn't get to it until late afternoon. I accepted that, thanked them, and hung up.

We had time to kill, and I asked Rue if he wanted to take a walk. I was heading to Tapper's office now that Mark Morrison had already identified LeAnn and left.

"Why are we going to pay Tapper a visit?"

"I've got a few questions for him."

"Sure. Let's go."

At our basement level, I knocked. Tapper called out to come in, then we entered his office.

A solemn look crossed his face. "Man, that never gets easier. The poor guy is completely broken."

"Yeah, I bet he is. Mind if we sit?"

Tapper pointed at the chairs facing his desk. "What's on your mind, Mitch?"

"Well, it's what you said the other day about the organs being removed carefully."

"Uh-huh."

"That's still bouncing around in my head. Were LeAnn's removed the same way as Valerie's? Carefully, I mean?"

"Her chest cavity wasn't butchered if that's what you're asking."

"Is there any way to tell if the same instrument, or knife, if you will, was used?"

"I can only say that the cuts were clean, so I'd say a very sharp knife was used in both cases."

"And that same knife was used in the kill wounds?"

"Probably. Sharp, deep cuts, but no way to identify the type. The cut pattern wasn't unique in any way as in having nicks in the blade, and it wasn't serrated."

"So a professional butcher knife or even a common hunting knife could have done the trick?"

"Honestly, yes, but the wounds were all about an inch wide if that helps."

I knuckled the desk and stood. Rue followed suit. "Okay, thanks, Tapper."

"You bet."

"So why did we go down there?" Rue asked as we walked the stairs back to our floor.

"Just wondering if we could tell the type of killer we're dealing with by the knife he used. Apparently not."

I wondered if calling in that profiler was still on Royce's mind. I also wondered if that person could actually help.

It was finally time to head to the mall. We stopped in to tell Royce we would be back in an hour. Even though a full day had passed since LeAnn had been abducted, we could get lucky and find something of evidentiary value in the area where she'd normally parked.

We arrived five minutes early, parked near the outer lot, and stood outside the cruiser like I'd told Margo we would. I tipped my chin at the car headed our way.

"That's got to be her," I said. "A shopper would park closer to the building."

The vehicle slowed, and a woman was driving. I waved to ease her mind. She rolled up next to us, lowered her window, and called out. I showed her my badge, then she thanked me and parked.

"You can never be too careful," she said after exiting her car. Margo extended her hand and shook ours.

I made the introductions and asked if we were in the right area.

"Close. We can just walk if you want to. It's over

there where that tree is by the curb." Margo pointed about fifty feet away.

We headed in that direction on foot, and I noticed Rue scanning the asphalt as he walked.

"Yeah, right here. LeAnn always parked next to the curbed peninsula so at least one side of her car would never get dinged up. Honestly, I never saw cars parked this far out except at Christmastime. I told LeAnn in the past that her car stood out like a sore thumb just because she parked so far from everyone else."

That comment made me think. I was sure the killers thought the same thing when they chose the owner of that car as their next victim. I was also sure there had to be two of them. One person working alone couldn't snatch, subdue, and restrain a victim and still drive away as fast as possible. We were looking for a killing team, and my mind again went to Jacob and Dylan, but I had to let go of that theory. They weren't good for the murders.

Margo stood silently for a minute, and I could see her wheels turning.

"Detectives, is it safe to work here?"

"I believe it is, and I also believe the only reason LeAnn ended up dead is because of where she parked. She was the lamb that strayed from the flock. As far as everything we can talk about and what we actually know, her death was absolutely a random act of violence."

Margo's voice cracked when she spoke. "I guess I better go park my car and get inside."

I handed Margo my card and thanked her for the help. "If anything else comes to mind, please call."

With a nod, she returned to her car.

I shielded my eyes and looked toward the building.

"What the hell was she thinking? That is a long way to walk alone at night."

Rue agreed. "It sure is, partner, and LeAnn paid the ultimate price to protect her new car."

"That's right, and Valerie paid the ultimate price, too, just to go to the bar Friday night. Look how far away she parked from Sparky's."

"Yep, they made themselves easy targets. Come on. Let's search a hundred feet out in every direction."

Devon and I spent a half hour searching the area. Other than disintegrating cigarette butts that looked to have been there for months, and two pennies, we didn't find anything we considered helpful.

Rue muttered under his breath. "Damn it. This is a waste of time. Those killers know how to cover their tracks well. Nothing rushed and nothing left behind."

"What are you saying?"

He swatted the air. "Thinking out loud, I guess. If the killers *are* selling the organs, wouldn't they have to rush? I mean, organs have a short shelf life, and obviously, the killers aren't the ones transplanting them into patients. They're the first line of the transaction."

I wiped away the sweat running down my cheeks. The black asphalt parking lot was intensifying the midday heat and made me feel like I was in a pressure cooker. The lack of shade didn't help either. I jerked my head toward the cruiser. "Come on. Let's discuss our theories in the air-conditioned car."

Back in the cruiser, I turned over the engine and pointed the vents of cold air toward me. Rue did the same on his side.

"Whew, that asphalt is no joke," I said. "So back to your theory. If the killers are selling organs, I'd agree that they only have a limited amount of time before those organs prove useless. The middleman wouldn't do business with them, though, if they were selling bad parts, so that means the go-between or end user has to be nearby."

"One would think so, but the last known cases of organ trafficking, according to the FBI, were in New York and California, and those people were arrested months ago," Rue said.

"Right, and the last busted ring in the South was in Atlanta in 2007." I raised a brow at Rue. "With a light plane, you could get to Atlanta in an hour and a half. I wonder if a new group has started up there. We need to find out what happened to those original traffickers and where they are now then have a word with them."

Devon nodded. "Do you think Royce will go for it?"

I sighed. "I guess we're going to find out. God knows we don't have any other leads."

I pulled out of the parking lot and told Rue to make the call. We needed to know if Royce was in his office and had time to talk to us about a possible trip to Atlanta.

Chapter 26

"What seems to be the problem?" Teddy asked after Chase hung up the phone.

"I'm not sure there is a problem. I mean, Mr. Harris didn't sound mad, but he said he needs to speak to us in person."

"So it's something important, then? Something he doesn't want to discuss over the phone?"

Chase scratched the top of his head. "Yeah, I guess. Anyway, let's go. We can't say no to our bread and butter. Not now, not ever."

"Yep, I'm ready to roll. We'll fill up the van, grab a couple of sandwiches and sodas at the gas station, and hit the highway."

If they left immediately, the brothers would make it to Augusta by five o'clock give or take a half hour depending on traffic. Mr. Harris wasn't expecting them to arrive before six. That would give them extra time in case anything went to shit before they reached the city limits.

They filled the van with gas and bought sandwiches

and snacks for the road, a six-pack of soda, and a bag of ice to keep their beverages cold in the cooler. With Chase behind the wheel, they were on their way and heading north by two thirty.

The next hour was filled with talk of their daydreams and plans—and music. Teddy passed a second soda to his brother and cracked a can open for himself. He glanced out the side mirror then spun in his seat. "Are you speeding?"

Chase looked at the speedometer. "Shit. I guess I was. Why?"

"Look out your side mirror. There's a highway patrol car coming up on us pretty fast."

Chase glanced out and cursed. "Damn it. We don't have time for this shit."

"That's it? That's what you're worried about? What about the ropes and eye bolts set up in the back? What about the bloody tarp that we haven't tossed yet? What about the bag with duct tape, zip ties, and gags in it? We're screwed, Chase." Teddy looked at the mirror again. "He just turned on his red and blues. You'll have to pull over. There's no way we can outrun him in this van." Teddy opened the console and pulled out the knife.

Chase's head nearly snapped off his neck. "What are you going to do with that?"

"Nothing unless I absolutely have to."

Gravel crunched under the van's tires as Chase pulled to the shoulder and set his flashers. They waited, likely while the cop ran the plates.

Chase looked through the mirror. "Stay calm. He's getting out and coming to your side, Teddy. Lower your window and hide that knife."

Teddy slipped the knife into the door pocket. As long as the brothers stayed cool, apologized, and accepted the speeding ticket, they should be on their way within ten minutes. If not, all hell would break loose.

Teddy watched through the mirror as the trooper walked to his door.

"Afternoon, gentlemen."

They nodded.

"Driver's license and registration, please."

Chase pulled his license from his wallet, and Teddy rifled through the glove box for the registration, then Teddy handed both to the officer.

"In a hurry to get somewhere?"

Chase took the reins. "Not really, sir. We're just enjoying the ride and listening to the radio. I'll admit, I wasn't watching the speedometer. My bad."

"I clocked you at ninety-two miles an hour. Where are you headed?"

"To Macon, where I live. Just went down to Savannah for a few days to visit my brother here, then he decided to come back with me for a while."

The trooper frowned. "This highway doesn't go to Macon."

"Sorry. I should have said we were going to visit cousins in Swainsboro first and then cut over to Macon." Chase gave the trooper his best smile.

"What's in the back?"

Teddy answered quickly. "Nothing, sir."

"No suitcases?"

Teddy stammered. "Um."

"I'll need both of you to step out of the vehicle."

With lightning speed, Teddy plunged the knife into the trooper's throat. He grabbed the officer's shirt so he would remain against the vehicle. Blood sprayed Teddy's face and the side of the van. There was no way to hide that.

"Open the sliding door! Hurry. We have to toss his ass inside, restrain him, and then pull off the highway onto some back road."

Chase jumped over the seat and yanked open the door. He removed the gun from the officer's holster and ripped the radio from his shoulder. He handed both to Teddy, then together, they secured the trooper to the ropes.

"I think he's good for now," Teddy said. "He'll be dead in a minute from blood loss." He looked back and saw there wasn't anyone coming. Teddy wiped his face on his sleeve the best he could, put on the trooper's hat, and grabbed the door handle. "Get going and turn off as soon as you can. I'll be right behind you." He leapt out of the van and ran back to the police car. He peeled out behind Chase and followed him several miles down the highway until he saw the van's right blinker turn on.

Finally. Now to find a place to ditch this police car, rip out the camera, and get the rest of that damn blood off me and the van.

Teddy followed closely as Chase got deeper and deeper into the back country. Several miles in, the roads turned from paved to gravel. That was a good sign, and hopefully, they would find an overgrown road with no indication it had been used by anyone. Chase slowed, and his brake lights flashed. He backed up until his window was alongside the police car. Teddy lowered the driver's window, making sure to press the button with his sleeve.

"What's up?"

Chase pointed. "That looks like a good spot. Pull in there and go as far as you can. That's where we'll leave the car."

Teddy turned right and drove in. Tangles of over-grown bushes and tree limbs scraped the sides of the trooper's car. He was sure they didn't have a lot of time to screw around. Police vehicles usually had tracking devices on them, and sooner or later, the car would be located. They needed to take the cameras, wipe down the car, and get the hell out of Dodge.

Chase followed in the van until Teddy stopped. They exited both vehicles with little room to move among the brush.

"Let's toss his ass in the trunk and wipe the blood off the van with some of the melted ice," Chase said.

"Wait. We can't throw away a perfect opportunity."

"Meaning?"

"Meaning, let's gut the guy. He's dead anyway, and why waste perfectly good organs? We have ice, and we can cut Mr. Harris a smoking good deal. He'll thank us for our generosity."

Chase shook his head. "How much time do you think we have? Shit, we don't even have a change of clothes in the van."

"Take off everything down to your skivvies. That way, you won't get blood on your clothes. We'll take what we have time to take then toss his remains in the brush. The animals will finish him off in no time."

"Okay, but we have to hurry."

Chase untied the trooper and placed him flat on the tarp they'd used for LeAnn. Teddy ripped the camera out of the car and wiped down everything he'd touched. He threw the keys into the brush then went to help Chase.

With the trooper lying naked in the back of the van, Teddy and Chase got busy. Using his knife, Teddy cut through the trooper's chest and opened his rib cage, where the valuables were located.

He jerked his head at Chase. "Take those sodas out

of the cooler then grab the baggies and foil from the supply box." Teddy carefully removed the heart and lungs then the liver and kidneys. That was all they needed. After the organs were put in plastic bags, wrapped in foil, and placed on ice, Teddy dipped the trooper's shirt into the cooler to soak up the water, washed his face with it, then cleaned the side of the van.

They carried the trooper's hollow body into the brush and tossed it as far as they could.

"Look around. Make sure you have all his clothes and belongings, every camera inside the car and out, the radio, and anything from the car that could lead back to us. You got rid of the keys, right?"

"Yep, they're gone."

Chase scanned the area. "Okay, put everything except his phone, badge, and wallet in that tarp and roll it up. We'll throw it in a dumpster somewhere in Augusta. The rest of the stuff will be tossed one piece at a time in different spots. Right now, we've got to get back on track. We have one hour before Mr. Harris expects us to be there."

Chapter 27

Back at the precinct and in Royce's office, we sat in the guest chairs and faced him. He asked how the white van search was going, and I said that Lawrence and Bentley had been working on it. The list had come in from the DMV only twenty minutes earlier. I suggested putting out a BOLO for white vans so Patrol could at least check out the driver if they came across one.

Royce tapped his fingers against his desk. "Okay, I'll pass that on. So what else is up other than the van? Find something at the mall parking lot?"

"Only that it was foolish for LeAnn to park that far away from other cars. Doing that put a target on her back."

"Hmm, sounds familiar. Isn't that the same way Valerie ended up dead, by parking away from everyone else at night?"

"Exactly. Even though they didn't realize it at the time, they were both complicit in their own abductions and deaths."

Royce agreed. "Sad but true. These days, people get too comfortable in their routine or in their false sense of security. Nobody thinks anything will happen to them."

Rue took his turn. "Until it does."

Royce knuckled his desk. "Okay, so?"

I glanced at Rue. "So, we were wondering about that last known organ-trafficking bust in Atlanta in 2007."

"Uh-huh. If I'm not mistaken, all of those players ended up in prison."

"Right, but that was fifteen years ago. I'm sure they're out and doing their own thing."

Royce stared at us. "I imagine they've served their time."

"What if they're up to no good again?" Rue asked.

"Human organs don't stay viable forever, Devon. One would think if somebody is going to sell organs in Atlanta, they'd do the killing there too. Makes more sense."

My eyes locked with Royce's. "Does it? The first people who would be blamed are the ones who committed those acts in the past, but if they were to kill and remove the organs from someone, say, five hours away, it wouldn't necessarily shine a light on them."

Royce rubbed his chin. "And a human heart only has about a five-hour shelf life."

"True, but what if the organs were flown from here to Atlanta in a private plane? The flight is less than an hour. It's completely doable."

"And that's a lot of speculation. Why are we discussing this anyway?"

"We'd like to track down those traffickers and find out what they're doing now."

Royce waved his hands. "You have no grounds whatsoever, only a theory. You can't hound, stalk, or try to make a case against people based on theories." He raised a brow at me. "How much time have you put into this idea of yours?"

"None yet."

"Good. Keep it that way. I'd suggest you two go help Bentley and Lawrence and then start over with Valerie. Review the police reports, talk to her friends again, interview everyone at the bars she frequented that night, and look at every minute of store footage that followed her as she walked the route to her car. Do exactly the same with LeAnn, and then and only then, if nothing or nobody surfaces, come talk to me again. I want every detective on every shift working this case."

He shooed us out and asked me to close the door. Rue and I walked to our office with our tails tucked between our legs.

"Wow, that didn't go the way I expected."

Rue let out a frustrated-sounding groan but said he understood Royce's point. "He can't let us go on every wild-goose chase, Mitch. We'd be leaving the others in the lurch while we're following our unfounded theories."

"Yeah, I guess. Let's get those vans knocked out and then see what fate throws our way."

We stopped in as we were passing Lawrence and Bentley's office.

"So how many white vans are actually registered in Chatham County?" I asked.

Bentley spoke up. "Many more commercial ones than privately owned ones."

That comment caught my attention. "Really? That sounds promising. The white blur that passed the mall camera didn't have any writing on the side."

Lawrence reminded me that many people used their vehicles for both personal and professional use by simply attaching a magnetic advertising panel to the side of the vehicle.

"Yeah, there is that. Anyway, how many do we have for personally registered vehicles?"

"Thirty-seven. I guess white family-size vans aren't a hot commodity. People like something a little less boring as a personal vehicle," Bentley said.

"Okay, let's dig in. How are you guys doing this?"

"By the plate number. That'll pull up the name of the registered owner, and then checking them for a police record is up to us."

"Sure, and how many have you done?"

Bentley tore the printed sheet of paper in half and handed me the lower part. "Knock yourselves out. So far, we don't have anyone with more than a parking ticket."

In our office, Rue and I got busy. I tore that same piece of paper in half again and passed the lower part over to him.

"We've only got seven plates each. After that, we'll have to start on the commercial list."

"Don't remind me. So, it sounds like tomorrow, we'll be starting from scratch. We'll have to reinterview everyone, and I guess the night shift guys will have to hit the bars if they want to talk to the people who worked on the Friday night Valerie was there. Between the four of us daytime detectives, we'll speak with her friends and relatives again then watch the footage from every camera on the route back to her car."

I grumbled. "Sounds like a waste of time to me. I mean, why chase something a second time that we've already done?"

"Because we're mere detectives and haven't reached the rank of sergeant yet."

I flipped Rue the bird and typed in the first license plate number.

Chapter 28

Teddy climbed out of the van and faced Chase. "How do I look?"

His brother laughed. "You aren't walking down the red carpet at the Academy Awards."

"I know, I know, but I don't want remnants of dried blood still on my face."

"You're fine. I'm fine, and we got here in time. I think Mr. Harris will forgive us if we aren't dressed to the nines."

"You literally just rhymed three words, bro."

Chase rolled his eyes and knocked on the door. Seconds later, a voice spoke through the wall-mounted camera.

"Come around to the side gate. We'll talk in the back."

Chase elbowed Teddy and pointed his chin toward the right side of the house. The home was large, fancy, and well-hidden by thick shrubbery and trees even though it was in an established neighborhood of upper middle-class homes.

"This is what I'm talking about." Teddy whistled under his breath. "You think we'll ever get to this point?"

"Only if we don't get caught or get too greedy. Apparently, if Mr. Harris can do it, we can too," Chase whispered. "There's the gate. Greet him politely and then shut up. Let him do the talking."

"Got it."

The gate swung inward, and Mr. Harris stood in front of the brothers. He'd never met Teddy before and looked him up and down before returning his attention to Chase. "Your brother?"

"Yes, sir. This is Ted, my right-hand man."

"Yeah, okay. Come in and have a seat on the patio. I've got a big private backyard, and nobody will hear our conversation. My cook is inside preparing supper."

"Understood, Mr. Harris."

"The reason I summoned you gentlemen is because my buyer is pleased with what you've provided so far. His contact wants to know if the amount of product can be doubled. He has a half-dozen buyers who are on a waiting list."

Teddy kept quiet and looked at Chase, who seemed to be weighing the risks. "It's possible, but we'd have to hit different cities throughout Georgia. We might be able to do two more jobs in Savannah, and then we'd have to go elsewhere. The risk would be too high there after that."

"So, is that a yes?"

"It's a yes, but we'd need a travel allowance since we'd be living out of hotels and eating on the go."

Mr. Harris smiled. "I like your bravado, Chase."

"Thank you, sir, and to show our appreciation of the business relationship we've established, we brought you a little something."

"Something for me?"

"That's right."

Chase nodded, and Teddy excused himself. Within minutes, he was back with the cooler. He placed it at their buyer's side.

"For you sir," Teddy said.

Chase interjected, "Everything in the cooler for twenty thousand as a token of our appreciation."

Mr. Harris opened the cooler and folded back the foil on one of the packages. He looked through the baggie and smiled. "Thank you. This is more than generous, and my buyers will be pleased. How old are the products?"

"Only an hour old," Chase said.

"Excellent. I'll make the call and fix us some drinks. I'll be right back with the cash."

Chase waited until the buyer was out of earshot before speaking. "Now that's how you keep your customers satisfied. Good idea, little bro."

Chapter 29

We had exhausted our search of all the white personal vans in Chatham County. None of the owners had police records worth taking a second look at. It was time to move on to the commercial vehicles, but first, we had to make sure none of their plates matched the ones on the personal vans. We didn't want to work twice as hard for half the effort. After crossing off nine vehicles that were multiuse vans, we ended up with 126 white commercial vans to research, and between the four of us, we decided to utilize the conference room to do it.

I rubbed my forehead before we began. Since it was after six o'clock and Royce would kick us out any second, we could leave the chore for morning and continue then, or we could let the night shift do it.

I pondered that question, then a realization struck me. "This doesn't work."

"What do you mean?" Bentley asked.

"The van in the mall footage didn't have any writing on the sides. How many white commercial vans have any of you seen that didn't have one ounce of advertising on them? I mean, that's why they're white. The vehicle literally gets used like a whiteboard for their business. If the van was a personal one that gets used for work, too, then we've already eliminated them."

"Humph," Lawrence said. "Then I guess we're done."

"And we didn't find any felons in that list or people who have spent a night in jail. I guess that angle went nowhere."

"It did, but it wasn't a waste of time," Rue said. "Everything we do is a process of elimination, and that gets us one step closer to learning who the perps are and where to find them."

I grunted. "If you say so. Come on. Let's update the night shift and get the hell out of here."

Royce and Bleu leaned against the wall of the conference room and listened in. We didn't have anything outstanding to report, so there wasn't an actual briefing between shifts. We told the night shift that the white van theory had been exhausted without any promising evidence to pursue, and it was time to move on.

With that said, Bleu told his detectives to go over Valerie's case again starting with a review of all the police reports and interview statements. They would visit the bars, speak to everyone again, then reinterview the two girls who were out with Valerie on Friday, the last night she was seen alive. If time permitted, they would watch the bar and store footage along the route to her car. By then, the night shift would be over with, and ours would begin again.

Rue and I clocked out and said good night in the parking lot. I was ready to put my legs up on the recliner, give my right one a much-needed rest, and drink a beer. I would try to follow Rue's practice of compartmentalizing things. Give everything that needed attention the attention it deserved then move on. I hoped by bedtime and with a couple of beers and a melatonin under my belt, my mind would be free of work thoughts, and I'd be ready for a good night's sleep. I planned to see if Rue's practice really worked or if I was too high-strung to actually follow through.

Once I got home and settled in for the night, I looked at the clock as I watched TV. I had two and a half hours before learning whether sleep would come easily and peacefully or not.

Breaking news interrupted the documentary we were watching about endangered species in the Serengeti. At first, I was irritated by the interruption, but I quickly sat up straight with my ears perked. The news report was about a missing state trooper in the Statesboro area. His patrol car's GPS had pinged deep in the brush on a dead-end road not far from US Highway 80, but he hadn't responded to numerous attempts to contact him. Since the Statesboro Sheriff's Office was the closest law enforcement agency to the trooper's vehicle, deputies were dispatched to the area.

"Oh my word," Mom said. "That's just terrible. Somebody probably killed the poor man."

I wagged my finger at her. "Why would you assume that, Mom? The search hasn't even begun, so don't speculate. I've done it plenty of times myself and have eaten crow more than I'd like to admit."

She grinned. "No, not you."

"Yep, me."

Marie piped in. "If the trooper's car was located in a really secluded place instead of on the highway like his job description says, and he's not responding to anyone, what could it be other than foul play?"

"Maybe it was planned and he wanted to disappear. Maybe he's sick of his job. Maybe he and his wife aren't getting along and he bailed on the marriage. Maybe he has a girlfriend that he left the state with. It could be anything."

"Including foul play," Mom said. "Aren't all police cars equipped with trackers?"

"Nah. It depends on the county and their budget for law enforcement equipment, but apparently his had a tracker. Anyway, open your mind to other possibilities. I'm sure to hear more about it tomorrow through the law enforcement channels." I smiled. "And I'll keep you two busybodies posted."

Chapter 30

A half-dozen deputies from the Statesboro Sheriff's Office tripped their way through the thick brush that moonless night, searching and calling out the trooper's name. The chirping cicadas were the only sounds they heard other than their own cursing.

Deputy Alan Carson grumbled. "I can't see shit out here even with the flashlight, and there's no room to move around. I keep falling over vines and downed branches."

"Same here," another deputy said.

They gathered back at the abandoned vehicle and looked through it for a second time. The keys, interior cameras, and radio were missing. Carson shined his flashlight at every location where exterior cameras were normally mounted. They were gone too.

"What the hell? Either he didn't want anyone to see what he was up to, or whoever brought his car back here didn't want the cameras to catch their actions." The deputy cupped his mouth and yelled out again but got nothing. "Let's head back to town and find out what we can from the state patrol about the trooper's route today, what channel he used to call in traffic stops, and what the last vehicle was that he pulled over. Maybe by listening to the radio transmissions he made, we'll get something. We've got to run everything by the captain, though, and he'll know what the next move should be."

The deputies returned to the sheriff's office and reported their findings to Captain Max Herman. The state patrol was immediately informed about what was and wasn't found at the scene. The trooper's vehicle had been located at the end of a gravel road. The deputies searched for the trooper, but after numerous attempts to locate him in the dark, brush-filled woods, they were unsuccessful. Every camera that could have recorded what happened in the secluded spot had been stripped off the vehicle, and the radio was gone too.

They were told that the state police would be on site first thing in the morning. During the night, they would listen to the trooper's recorded traffic stops to see if they could garner any information from them. The scene was to be manned by deputies throughout the night, and at first light, the state police would meet with them there.

Since the trooper's wife had already been notified and had given her statement, more information, including his name and photograph, would air every hour on every news station throughout Georgia. The news would also be forwarded to every police department in the state. Somebody had to know what had happened and where the trooper disappeared to, and according to the state police, foul play couldn't be ruled out.

Chapter 31

After retreating to my bedroom and realizing I wasn't tired yet, I clicked on the TV. It was a habit I'd tried to break many times since it was usually during the ten o'clock news that I found myself in bed and watching the most recent bad news the TV stations could muster up. Thinking about those unfortunate situations usually kept me awake much longer than I wanted.

I promised myself I'd watch the first segment then turn it off and try to sleep. Tomorrow was going to be a busy day of retracing our steps in the Valerie Dawson and LeAnn Morrison cases. Hopefully, somebody would come forward and tell us something that they hadn't disclosed earlier. I wondered if we should air their murders on the news. We would omit the gruesome details, yet everyone who knew the women already knew they had died.

I groaned and returned my focus to the TV. The commercial break had just ended, and the news was beginning with an update about that missing state trooper. They showed a picture of him and stated his name. That told me the family had already been interviewed and knew he was missing. The broadcast also mentioned that the radio and every camera the car was equipped with had been torn out.

Hmm, maybe he didn't disappear on his own accord or, like I thought before, stage his own disappearance. Yet to tear out all of the cruiser cameras and the radio seems pretty extreme. Either he was up to no good and bailed, or somebody else was and made him disappear.

"Damn it. Why did I turn on the TV at all? Now I'm going to play out different scenarios about the missing trooper. His car was found near Statesboro, though. Not our county, not our problem."

I knew I was kidding myself since law enforcement was a brother- and sisterhood of officers who always helped each other when called on. I also knew that trouble usually seemed to head our way.

I closed my eyes and, after a half hour, drifted off. The next time I opened them, it was morning. I was thankful that I had slept through the night—something that didn't often happen.

The aroma of freshly brewed coffee filled the hallway outside my bedroom door. I would grab a cup, take it upstairs, and listen to the news as I showered and dressed for work. I met up with Marie in the kitchen. She was cracking eggs into a bowl, which made the breakfast menu obvious—scrambled eggs and some form of meat, I assumed. My choice, if given one, was always bacon.

"Morning, sis."

Marie glanced my way and tipped her head toward the pantry. In code, that meant I was supposed to follow her. I noticed Chloe sitting at the dining room table, already busy with some kind of construction-paper-and-marker art project.

"What's up?" I asked once we were out of earshot of my niece.

"I had the TV on this morning, but when Chloe came down, I shut it off. They found that trooper."

"Yeah, and?"

"And he's dead, Mitch."

I furrowed my brows and whispered, "No shit?"

"No shit." Marie craned her neck to make sure Chloe was still at the table. "They didn't go into details on TV, but it had to be bad. There were dozens of news vans out on the main road, and the reporter said the state police feared foul play was involved."

"Damn. Did anyone say where he was found?"

"I guess right there where his car was located. Something about the darkness last night and the amount of brush made finding him impossible. They went out to search again this morning at first light and found him within thirty minutes."

"Okay, thanks for the heads-up. Let's not discuss anything during breakfast. Make sure Mom knows to keep it to herself. After what our family has gone through, news like that only upsets the girls."

"I know that far too well," Marie said.

I poured myself a cup of coffee and headed for the stairs. "I'll be down in twenty."

In my bedroom and with the door closed, I turned on the TV and immediately saw the broadcast. States-boro was just over an hour from Savannah, so the news was likely playing on every local channel. Especially in unsolved homicide cases, the manner of death wasn't disclosed to anyone in the media. Law enforcement and their associates were the only people who knew the truth. Family members often weren't told either until the perp was in custody and charged with the offense. I wondered if the manner of death had made it to the Savannah PD yet or if the state police and the Statesboro Sheriff's Office were keeping tight-lipped about it. I would know soon enough because if anyone had been told, it would be Royce.

I didn't linger long after breakfast. With food and two cups of coffee under my belt, and one cup to go, I said goodbye and headed out the door. If the precinct was abuzz with gossip when I got there, that would tell me the station had heard about the trooper, and Royce would share what he knew at our morning update.

At seven forty-five, I walked into the building. Diane greeted me with a somber nod. It was obvious that she had heard the news but not yet obvious whether anyone knew the details. I nodded back then continued to the stairs and up to our floor.

The buzz was definitely loud and sounded like a tree of cicadas. As I passed the lunchroom, I saw Royce and Rue leaning against the back counter, each with a coffee in hand. I backed up three paces and walked in.

"What's the latest?" I asked. Nobody needed to wonder what I was talking about—the news was etched on every face.

Royce groaned. "It isn't good, Cannon. We have bits and pieces of sketchy information. Not sure if the state police are ready to share details yet or not."

"Well, apparently they're not. Otherwise, we'd know."

"I believe they're waiting for the manner of death from the county coroner before making it official, and even then, the public isn't going to be told, at least not for a while."

"Standard practice. Do we know anything?"

"Only that the trooper was killed last night in a

violent manner and that every bit of potential evidence was removed from the scene."

"How about Forensics?"

Royce glanced at the wall clock. "The meeting is in five minutes, and I don't want to repeat everything twice. We'll have questions at the end of the briefing, and I'll answer everything to the best of my knowledge then."

I grabbed a coffee and walked downstairs with Royce and Rue. It looked like everyone was already in attendance from our night shift crew to the daytime personnel, including our beat cops. Royce wasted no time in stepping up to the podium. The morning briefing was usually a joint effort between Royce and Bleu, but because the news had just come in over the wire, Royce did all the talking. What he said was new information for everyone.

"Okay, okay, let's quiet down and get rolling so I can answer a few questions at the end."

A hush came over the room, and all eyes were on him. He clenched his hand into a fist and cleared his throat before beginning.

"The news last night spoke of an unaccounted-for state trooper who wasn't responding to his radio calls. His car was tracked to an overgrown road just outside Statesboro, where deputies were tasked to go search for him. When they arrived, they didn't find the trooper, only his abandoned car minus the radio and every camera. They said there wasn't any blood on or in the vehicle, and although they called out and searched with flashlights, they couldn't locate him." Royce paused for a drink of water then continued. "The state police were informed, and this morning, a joint search at the scene between them and the sheriff's office took place. The trooper's body was recovered from within the deep, tangled brush. The manner of death hasn't been officially released, so I don't want to hear watercooler speculation. All we know is that it was deemed a homicide, but there's no camera footage to show what happened. The state police retrieved the radio recording of the last known traffic stop and are processing that information. As of right now, that's all we have. I imagine the state police are taking charge, and everyone else is on a need-to-know basis. From what's been passed on, the coroner will give his official report to the state police this afternoon. Either we'll find out more through the grapevine, or we won't be privy to that information. It isn't our county, and Statesboro has their own police force and sheriff's office."

Royce opened up the room for questions. I wondered how many he would get thrown at him since he had already explained that he didn't know anything more than what he'd just told us.

Bentley spoke up first. "Are the state police trying to keep the results from Forensics and the coroner hush-hush? Meaning it's their case and they don't want anyone else in on it?"

Royce held up his hands. "I don't know, Curt. I haven't worked a case with the state police in a decade. I'm sure many of them are different people than the ones I knew back then, and besides that, we aren't first in line to be told anything."

I took a shot at Royce and asked the question I was going to ask him earlier. "What about Forensics? Did they find anything at the scene? Maybe even a second set of tire tracks?"

"Not to my knowledge, or at least nothing I've heard. The patrol car is being processed at the Bulloch County evidence garage."

"And what about the audio recording of the last traffic stop?" Rue asked.

"I did hear that there were sound issues. Garbled communications that the sheriff's office tech department is working on." Royce looked around. "If that's it, then let's get rolling. We've got a busy day ahead of us, but if anything else comes to light, it'll be announced later at shift change."

Rue and I hung back until the room cleared. Royce and Bleu were discussing the trooper's death when we approached them.

"Excuse us," I said, "but do you want us to start on Valerie's case and retrace everything that's already been done?"

"Yep, that's the plan."

I looked at Sergeant Bleu. "Did the night shift guys talk to the bar employees last night?"

"They did. Sounds like the statements were the same as before, and nobody had anything new to offer."

I tipped my head. "Okay, thanks. We'll talk to Valerie's friends and family again while Bentley and Lawrence review all of the footage that was collected."

Rue and I headed to our office to gather the transcripts of police interviews we'd had with everyone Valerie knew or was related to. We would try again and hope for a name we hadn't gotten before.

Devon dropped into his chair then spoke up. "So what do we do about Jacob, Dylan, and all those cult nutjobs who spent time in jail for animal abuse? Are we to assume they aren't involved, or do we interview them again too?"

I shrugged. "Let's talk to the normal people first and see if we make any headway before we decide."

"Works for me. Let's pay Valerie's family a visit first."

Rue and I drove to the home where Valerie had lived with her parents. This would be our first face-to-face with Mr. and Mrs. Dawson. When it was confirmed that the woman found in the marsh was indeed Valerie, Morrow and Mason had paid her parents the unfortunate initial visit. Maybe our questions and their answers would be somewhat different than what our weekend detectives had discussed with them. We would also talk to some of the dayshift employees at the bars Valerie and her friends had frequented that fateful Friday night. Daytime employees could also know sketchy characters who stopped in often. Any one of those people could have returned during the late-night hours and chosen Valerie as the person to follow to her car.

"I was just thinking about the similarities in Valerie and the trooper's cases."

I glanced at Rue as I waited for the green light. "In what way?"

"Well, it was mentioned that the last traffic stop the trooper conducted was the one that mattered. Same goes for Valerie. It's only the last bar and what happened when it closed that matters. She was never seen alive again after leaving Sparky's."

"True enough. Then Delilah's and The Grinch don't hold much relevance. After we talk to Valerie's folks and her friends, we'll interview the afternoon crew at Sparky's to see if they can shed more light."

Fifteen minutes later, we stood on the porch and knocked on the door of the Dawson home. After Nancy, the wife, answered, we explained who we were and why we were there. It was true that we didn't have anyone in custody, and the family knew it. We didn't have a suspect either, yet we needed their help. It was time to dig deep, even if that meant taking Valerie's room apart and looking for clues. Maybe we would find the names of people who had never come up before.

Mr. and Mrs. Dawson listed every person they could think of, good or bad, who had crossed paths with Valerie over the last year or two. While they worked on that, they allowed Rue and me to look through Valerie's bedroom. Her murder was so recent that they didn't want anything in the room to change or be mishandled since the bedroom was a place she'd always considered her sanctuary.

Rue and I searched drawers, boxes, Valerie's closet, and under the bed. We didn't find so much as a journal, a letter, pictures with unknowns in them, or a single scrap of paper with a name that hadn't been brought up before.

We sat with her parents and asked more questions. How often did she go out with her friends? Was it always to the same places, in the same order, at the same time of night? Those could be clues that would help us. Somebody, unbeknownst to her, might have been stalking her for days, weeks, or even months. That person could be someone who was infatuated with her and she'd never realized it.

"Several years ago, there was a bartender at Delilah's who was interested in her. They had a three-week fling, but when she found out he was engaged to a young lady who lived in Port Wentworth, she dumped him. He wasn't too happy about it, made idle threats for a while, then finally moved on. We'd heard that the girlfriend ended the engagement and the guy moved to Oregon."

"And his name?"

Mr. Dawson scrunched his face. "His name started with an *M*." He looked at his wife. "Do you remember, honey?"

"Um, it was something different. Marlon, maybe."

"Would Sherry Lyman remember him?"

"Probably."

"Okay, thank you, and we'll be in touch. Have you planned Valerie's funeral service yet?"

Mrs. Dawson's eyes welled up. "Yes, it'll be on her birthday, next Wednesday."

Chapter 32

We left the Dawson home and headed directly to Sherry Lyman's house, which was within walking distance of my own. Luckily, she was still home and hadn't left yet for her part-time job.

We reviewed her original statement with her and needed to know if anything had changed, if she was mistaken about any details, or if any new memories had surfaced. She said that what she had explained during the first interview was accurate and fresh in her memory at that time.

"Sherry, do you remember the bartender that Valerie was seeing briefly a few years back? She dumped him when she found out he was engaged. A Marlon or something like that?"

She nodded. "Yep, I remember that jerk. His name was Marten, with an *e*—Marten Hambrecht—and he said he was Dutch. He bartended at Delilah's for a year and totally thought he was hot shit."

I jotted the name down on the back of the folder containing Sherry's original statement.

"That must have been after you ladies all turned twenty-one," Rue said.

"It was, and we wanted to go out, party, and see how it felt to do exactly what we wanted to do legally. We were all of age."

I smiled. "Yep, reaching twenty-one is a big deal."

Sherry huffed. "I think it's way overrated. What it means is that you're legally of age to do whatever you want, but that comes with a lot of responsibility too."

"No truer words," Rue said.

"Did Val and Marten part ways on a bad note?" I asked.

"Yeah, and then his fiancée broke up with him. He was really pissed, but he brought it on himself."

"We hear he moved to Oregon," I said. "Has he ever come back to Savannah that you know of?"

She frowned as if she was thinking. "No, not to my knowledge anyway."

"And the fiancée lived in Port Wentworth?"

"Yes, with her sister."

"Do you know if the sister or the fiancée still lives there, and their names?"

"I never met either of them, but Val heard that the fiancée's name was Patrice Doocy."

"Okay, great. So nobody else who strikes you as weird that you forgot to mention?"

"No, and nobody creeped us out that night either. I don't think it was anyone from the bar scene who killed Val, though."

"Why do you say that?" Rue asked.

Sherry pulled a tube of lip balm from her pocket and ran it across her lips. "Just a gut feeling. It was a regular night at all three bars. Nothing was off until after we parted ways for the night."

"Then I guess that's it for now." I turned toward the door. "Oh, by the way, do you know anyone who owns a white van?"

She wrinkled her forehead. "No, can't say that I do."

"Okay, thanks again, and we appreciate your help. We'll show ourselves out."

Back at the cruiser, Rue flashed a raised brow at me.

"What?"

"I thought the white van theory was a dead issue."

"It still doesn't hurt to ask."

"Whatever. So are we going to hit Sparky's or look for the ex-fiancée?"

I checked the time. "Sparky's doesn't open until noon. Let's head to the precinct, look up that Marten character, and see if he has any priors. Oregon is a long way off to jump to conclusions."

Rue called Bentley and set his phone to Speaker as I drove. "Anything on the footage that you caught now but missed days ago?"

"Nope. There isn't a damn thing that stands out. In my opinion, we're spinning our wheels, but don't tell Royce I said that. How about you guys?"

"We got one name from Valerie's parents. Not sure if he's worth investigating or not. We'll see if he has any priors first and then take it from there." Rue hung up and looked at me. "If that Marten guy isn't worth checking out, then we're back to having nothing, and I'm sure it'll be the same with LeAnn. Is there anything Royce would consider airing on TV?"

I shook my head. "We don't have a perp profile, a motive, or a vehicle to tell the public about. You know damn well Royce's next move will be that FBI profiler, and I just don't know how much he can help."

"Well, that's Royce's call, but when it's all said and done, we'll be the ones who solve this case."

I chuckled. "I like your optimism."

"Not optimism. It's just based on facts. We're working this investigation every hour, not them. The FBI doesn't have a dog in this fight and won't unless there's proof that the organs are being sold and transported over state lines. Right now, there's no proof that either is happening. It's highly unlikely that the FBI is the agency who will find that out."

I frowned. "Sounds like the FBI leaves a bad taste in your mouth."

He swiped away my comment. "Nah, just don't take the credit when no credit is due."

I parked in our lot, and we entered the building. "Now, let's find out who Marten Hambrecht really is."

I was grasping at straws and knew it. The likelihood of an ex-boyfriend murdering Valerie was small. He'd had a brief relationship with her and moved across the country two years back. The only thing that could set someone like him off was the fact that his fiancée had dumped him when she found out he was cheating. Maybe there was some potential financial gain to marrying her that had gone up in smoke, yet the fact that he was cheating also meant the fiancée didn't hold a high place in his heart. Killing LeAnn, too, wouldn't make sense at all. She didn't have anything to do with him, his fiancée, or Valerie.

Like Bentley said, we were spinning our wheels. We couldn't force our narrative to become fact, but we would look up Marten's name in the criminal database anyway. I was sure he would be checked off our list before lunchtime.

First, I typed his full name into the Savannah police

records to see if he'd ever been arrested locally, and he hadn't. After that, I searched the nationwide criminal database, which quickly eliminated his name—he was nowhere to be found in the system. Marten Hambrecht wasn't our man.

I was disappointed but not surprised. I wouldn't bother mentioning Marten to Royce since he'd already thought we were wasting time when I suggested tracking down the organ traffickers who were arrested in 2007.

Leaning back in my chair, I let out a long groan and stretched. I was getting the midday slumps and needed a caffeine boost. I rose and walked to the door.

"Need a coffee?"

"Yeah, but I'll tag along. A walk might perk me up."

I laughed. "You mean a snack from the vending machine might perk you up?"

"Hey, as long as I'm in there anyway."

In the lunchroom, we met up with Lawrence, who looked to have the same idea. He was plugging change into the coffee machine.

"Running on empty?" I asked.

"Feels like it, although Royce said he heard more about the trooper incident. That perked me up for a few minutes."

"How did you learn something from Royce?"

Lawrence waved off my comment. "Don't get your panties in a bundle. He was just in here and mentioned it as he was waiting for his coffee cup to fill."

"What did he say?"

"Something about the radio transmission cutting out when the trooper called in the plate number of the last vehicle he pulled over before he fell off everyone's radar."

"So they obviously didn't get the plate number, or the

state police would already have the owner of that vehicle detained for questioning."

"Sounds about right."

"And that's all they had to work with?"

"Don't know. It's the only thing Royce mentioned."

"Hmm."

"What?"

"I need to run something by Royce that could work. Just depends on if he wants to offer his input or not."

When we left the lunchroom, Rue asked what I was talking about.

"I'll tell you both at the same time, but it does go back to the last vehicle the trooper pulled over as being the only one that mattered."

Rue chuckled. "Okay, let's see if Royce is open to your idea this time since the Atlanta thing didn't go over very well."

After I gave Royce's open door a courtesy knock, we were waved in. "What's up?"

"Well, we met up with Lawrence in the lunchroom, and he said you'd heard that the trooper's radio transmission on the last vehicle he pulled over didn't go through properly. What was important, the vehicle plate number, was garbled."

Royce shrugged. "That's what Patrol passed on. They heard it from the Bulloch County highway deputies." He cocked his head and waited. "So?"

"So, depending on whether the state police want ideas or help, I thought of something they can do."

"And you don't think they've already thought of everything?"

"Don't know, Boss, but if they didn't, it might help."

Royce groaned. "You do know this isn't our priority. Chatham County is."

"Okay, never mind."

I stood, then Royce pointed at the chair. "Just tell me already so I can get back to work. What's eating at you?"

"We already know that the trooper's car had a tracking system on it. That's how the deputies were able to locate it."

"Correct."

"Then they should be able to see exactly where the vehicle was during that last traffic stop, what time it was there, and how long it took before the vehicle moved off the highway and into the woods. They wouldn't need his radio transmission to figure that out, right?"

"That's right. So?"

"So, since they have nothing else to work with and if they can pinpoint his exact location and the exact time he pulled that last car over, then they could air that on the news and ask for help from people who passed that location at that time. Plenty of people drive the highways, and any number of them could have noticed that state trooper as he sat along the shoulder with a vehicle pulled over in front of him. If an alert passerby paid attention, they could call in the color and type of vehicle they saw. It could be a start." I looked at Royce and tried to read his face. It was contorted.

"We aren't involved in the case, Mitch. Nobody has asked for our help, and one-upping the state police about something they might not have thought to do would put them in a bad light."

I swatted the air. "Let them take the credit. They probably would have anyway. Isn't finding that trooper's killer the important thing here, not outsmarting other law enforcement officials?"

Royce blew out a puff of air. "Of course it is, but approaching them with that idea is the hard part."

"Excuse me, Boss, but you are a homicide sergeant in a relatively large city. I think you have some credibility."

Royce chuckled. "Well, thanks."

I turned to Rue. "What do you think?"

"I think why not? The public has helped out law enforcement many times. That's why perp profiles are always aired on the news. Right now, nobody knows who the perp is, so it'll take forever to piece the clues together. Learning what kind of vehicle the trooper pulled over and having that lead to an arrest will be huge."

I saw the wheels turn in Royce's head. Maybe he would get the credit after all for such a brilliant idea. His police station and the hardworking individuals there might get recognized. There wasn't a good reason to pass up a nod like that, but even more important, there wasn't a good reason to let a killer roam free.

"Okay, I'll make the call to the state police."

Rue and I grinned. It was the right thing to do, and with any luck, somebody would call in with the vehicle's description.

"So?"

I shrugged. "So what?"

"So why are you still sitting here? Get out so I can make the call."

We stood and walked out the door. I would have loved to listen in, but I knew Royce wanted to make the call privately. I was anxious, though, to find out whether the state police would act on the suggestion or not.

Chapter 33

Teddy paced the living room. "Do you really think we can live up to Mr. Harris's request without messing up?"

"Of course we can, especially if we move around and especially if he and his buyer are footing our travel expenses. Nobody will ever put two and two together. We don't even have to use my van all the time. We'll rent a different-colored one now and then to keep people from connecting the dots."

"Yeah, good plan." Teddy cracked open two cans of soda and placed them on the table next to the lunch he'd prepared. They each had two ham-and-cheese sandwiches—double slices of meat and cheese on both—and a bowl of corn chips sat centered on the table with dishes of salsa and guacamole next to it.

"So, are we going to harvest more organs here or move on?"

"I'll think about it. We've used the van three times already."

"Only twice locally, though."

With a mouthful of food, Chase nodded. "Good

point. Nobody will ever connect that trooper's death to us."

"But it was aired all over the news stations, and they found his car pretty quickly."

"We took every bit of evidence with us, and it's a good thing we did. We're good, bro. We'll mix up the towns, the vehicles, and the times we go out hunting. We're invisible, and we'll stay that way."

Teddy laughed. "Until we get that luxury boat. Being invisible is the last thing I want to do then. We're going to flaunt our good fortune."

"And it'll come, brother. Just be patient."

Teddy's phone alarm went off. "Time to hit the shower and get ready for work."

"Give them your notice already. When we're moving from town to town, you can't be working anyway. What we're doing is your job and pays a hell of a lot better than the one you have."

Teddy jammed a handful of chips into his mouth and left the table.

Chase yelled out after him. "I'll need that work schedule I asked for so we can plan our next job! Bring it home with you later."

Teddy flashed a thumbs-up as he disappeared down the hallway.

Chapter 34

It was after lunch, and Sparky's was open. Since Royce didn't want us to sit in on his conversation with the state police, we decided to head out.

We needed to interview the weekday manager and see if there were different employees working whom we hadn't spoken to yet. The more people we talked to the better chances of finding someone who knew of an oddball who frequented the bar.

The normal bar patron liked to socialize, drink, and watch sports. The sketchy ones liked to watch women— and not necessarily with good intentions in mind.

I had a list of every employee we'd talked to at every bar, but focusing entirely on Sparky's was the right thing to do. Even though Sherry didn't think the perp was someone who had been watching them from inside, we still needed to know who, if anyone, seemed to irritate the female patrons.

After walking in, we bellied up to the bar and ordered a couple of sodas from Justin. We hadn't seen him on Sunday when we were there talking to George and T. J., and getting another person's point of view was always good.

"So, Justin, how's business?"

"Slow today as far as tourists go, but the locals always come in for lunch."

I looked around and saw a dozen people with baskets of burgers and fries in front of them at the bar tables. Two men sat across the horseshoe-shaped bar, drinking beer and making small talk with T. J. He glanced over as he filled their glasses, and I gave him a wave.

He nodded and called out to us. "Holy cow, we've got the PD stopping by twice in one week." He chuckled. "We must have the best soda in town."

I grinned and leaned in toward Justin. "Is George the only manager or just the weekend manager?"

"Mostly the weekend unless he's filling in. Otherwise, it's Dottie."

"Is she here?"

"Yep. Do you want to talk to her?"

"We do, but first, we'd like to talk to you."

"Yeah, sure. Is it about that girl who was here on Friday night and wound up dead?" He pointed his thumb over his shoulder. "T. J. told us you were here on Sunday asking about her."

"Can you think of anyone who shines around that seems kind of off? Like they aren't here just to enjoy being at the bar?"

"You mean like a creeper? A guy who's looking for someone to hit on?"

"Worse than that," Rue said. "A *real* creeper. Someone who's possibly dangerous."

"Wow. I've never come across anyone like that, but I just work during the day. The real creepers probably come out at night when the bar is hopping. They blend in with the crowd, and that way, nobody realizes what their real intentions are."

I raised a brow. "That makes sense. So nobody comes to mind? No women complaining, maybe lunch customers?"

"Sorry, but no. T. J. is the right guy to ask. He works whenever somebody calls in sick or has a day off. Day or night, he's usually available."

I nodded a thanks. We would ask again, but T. J. had already told us what he knew when we spoke to him on Sunday. I asked Justin to let Dottie know we had a few questions for her. He disappeared down the hall, and T. J. strolled over.

"Need refills, Detectives?"

"Sure, thanks," I said. "So, no creepers come to mind that you couldn't think of when we spoke to you on Sunday?"

T. J. scratched his chin then shook his head. "Well, if we're calling this mystery person a creeper, there is Donny Pearson."

I frowned. "Donny Pearson? Isn't he, like, fifty?"

"Late forties, I think, but he's a strange one."

"How so?"

T. J. shrugged. "Doesn't talk much unless there's ladies in the bar. Then he becomes real chatty."

"That doesn't sound strange to me," I said.

Rue laughed. "Me either."

T. J. swatted the air. "Not in a normal way, guys. He's a real creeper. He makes the ladies feel uncomfortable. They've complained plenty about his disgusting innuendos."

"Hmm, so why didn't you mention him on Sunday?"

"Guess I thought you had a young guy in mind. Donny didn't fit that description, but he is a weird one."

"Okay, thanks."

T. J. headed to the other side of the bar and waited on several customers who had just sat down. I jerked my chin toward the hall, where Dottie was coming our way. After introducing ourselves to her, I explained why we were there and promised to keep the questions short and to the point. We had Donny Pearson to check into.

"I'm sure by now, you've heard about Valerie Dawson, who was found dead last weekend."

Dottie nodded.

"She left here at bar closing Friday night and was never seen alive again."

"Yes, what a tragedy."

"We've been asking around, and T. J. just told us about how Donny Pearson makes unwanted advances toward women. Were you aware of that?"

She sighed deeply. "I am, but I try to brush it off as him being socially awkward."

"May I ask why?"

"Because I don't want to antagonize him, and I don't want the ladies to stop coming in. I'm sure the night crew has far more problems to deal with than I do. I can't whine all day about Donny."

Rue glanced at me. "But does Donny show up at night too?"

Dottie cocked her head. "Donny is Donny. He lives on his disability check, so he can show up whenever he wants."

The more I heard, the more I doubted that Donny was our man. The killer would have to be physically capable of apprehending and quickly silencing screaming and kicking women. But we did think there was the chance there was more than one killer committing the murders and removing the organs. We would talk to Donny anyway since it was the prudent thing to do. We thanked Dottie, Justin, and T. J. then left.

I felt my phone vibrate as we headed to the station. I dipped my hand into my pocket and passed the phone over to Rue, who read the text then paraphrased it out loud.

"Humph. It sounds like the state patrol is actually going ahead with Royce's suggestion."

I coughed into my fist. "Whose suggestion?"

"Yeah, okay, your suggestion, but Royce was the conduit who got the message through."

"That's true." I laughed. "Good on Royce, but as usual, it's wait and see. The question is, will Royce be kept in the loop or not?"

"Time will tell. I'm anxious to find out if Donny has been arrested in the past, and if so, for what," Devon said.

"Well, we'll know in ten minutes or less if we're going to pay him a visit or not."

We entered the building and nearly slammed into Royce running down the stairs.

"Where's the fire?" I yelled out.

"Follow me."

Rue and I turned and followed on Royce's heels. Seconds later, he burst through Tapper's office door.

"What the hell is going on?" I asked.

Tapper sat behind his desk and waved us over. "This literally hit my in-box five minutes ago. It was copied to the handful of coroners in the counties that surround Bulloch County."

We stood at Tapper's back and read the autopsy report and cause of death for the trooper found in the brush at the end of that gravel road.

I couldn't believe what I was reading and had to read it a second time.

"Why wasn't this information passed on to us?" Royce asked.

Tapper shook his head. "Did you pass on the details about Valerie and LeAnn to every city police force and county sheriff's office?"

"No, but we didn't want the manner of death to get out. That was the ace up our sleeves in case some nutjob wanting his fifteen minutes of fame confessed to their murders."

"And the state police likely insisted on a gag order through Bulloch County so the trooper's manner of death didn't get out either. The county medical examiner doesn't work for the police or sheriff's department, and that's likely why he shared the information with other coroners. Somebody will make a statement to the media, but you know darn well they aren't going to disclose the real manner of death to the public."

"So what actually killed the trooper before his organs were removed?" I asked.

Tapper pointed at the second paragraph of the report. "The trooper's right carotid artery was severed by a knife. He bled out quickly, I'm sure. The press will probably be told he was killed by a knife wound and nothing more."

My forehead wrinkled. "That makes no sense to me. A killer wouldn't lure a state trooper to their vehicle just to kill him. Plus, they'd have to have something with them to preserve the organs until they're sold to the buyer."

Tapper pulled back. "So that's the theory? We're going with selling organs for profit?"

Royce let out a groan. "It's the only thing that seems

logical, yet nothing about the trooper scenario sounds logical at all. Do those killers drive around with a murder kit and a cooler full of ice at all times? That's absolutely crazy. If that's the case, then the buyer has to be within driving distance." Royce looked at me. "Obviously, the Atlanta theory doesn't work. Otherwise, the killer would have flown out of Savannah."

I had to agree. We still had Donny to check out, but that could come later. Royce was beside himself, and his beet-red face told me he was about to blow. He thanked Tapper and asked him to keep the information to himself, then we left. Royce needed a meeting of the minds with Bleu and all the detectives, and the sooner the better.

It was closing in on shift change anyway, and we had just enough time for the five of us to discuss the best course of action.

In my opinion, Royce had to let the state police in on the two deaths in Chatham County and how the women were found. In many ways, working hand in hand with the state police was better than working with the FBI. We were all local to Georgia and wouldn't have big shots in suits coming in from Manassas and taking over our cases. Bulloch County was next to Chatham County, and we had good reason to believe that the killer or killers in all three murders were the same people. The city, county, and state law officials had a tighter connection with each other than they had with the FBI. Their help was appreciated when necessary, but we were all confident that Georgia law enforcement officials, at least in this situation, could solve the three cases ourselves.

We'd made a plea to the public, too, about the chance sighting of the vehicle the trooper had pulled over. Having that information could help tremendously.

"We have more positives than negatives," I said. "The night crew can interview Donny just to check him off the person of interest list, but I really don't think he's involved."

Royce spoke up. "Now that we know about the condition of the trooper's body, and after we discuss the situation with the night crew, we'll have to let the state police and Bulloch County know that our two murder victims were found the same way. Not only are the perps murdering people and likely selling human organs, they're also considered serial killers. It doesn't matter that the body parts may go to a good cause in the end. Those perps are killing random people for a big payday and without a second thought."

Among our shift, we agreed to join forces with the state police and Bulloch County, but we needed Bleu's opinion and the opinion of his detectives too. It would be a group decision or the plan wouldn't go forward.

Earlier, Royce had texted Bleu to meet us in the second-floor conference room. We needed to speak with him and his detectives. His return message said he was on his way and that he would forward Royce's message to the guys. They'd be showing up soon.

Ten minutes later, and one by one, they walked in. Bleu must have stressed the importance of getting to the precinct and heading directly to the conference room. Everyone's expressions told us that they had no idea what the meeting was about.

Once they were seated and settled, Royce began with the news that Tapper had shared about the trooper.

Bleu was furious. "So nobody at the Bulloch County Sheriff's Office thought to share that information with other branches of law enforcement?"

Royce held up his hands. "Take a breath, Chuck. It

isn't like we shared information with anyone else either. Hell, we don't even have a suspect profile to share. The less the public knows about organ trafficking, the better. If we go off half-cocked with that news, it'll scare the shit out of everyone, plus we won't have that proverbial ace up our sleeves. Only the killer and us know that the bodies had been emptied of their salable organs. As of right now, we know how the trooper was found, but Bulloch County and the state police have no idea that the two murder victims we have in Chatham County were found the same way."

"So what's the suggestion? Why the meeting?"

Royce blew out a long breath. "We need to team up, a joint effort between all law enforcement agencies that are currently involved."

I took my turn. "Between us, we think it's the prudent thing to do, but we need everyone to be in agreement before we consider going forward."

Bleu looked at Royce then asked his detectives what they thought.

Prentice spoke up. "I don't think we have another choice. The main goal is to apprehend those maniacs, not to put a notch on our belts for doing everything alone. We've been working this case for damn near a week and aren't any further ahead than we were when Valerie was discovered."

Bleu nodded at Bloom. "Ricky?"

"I agree. Let's team up with the others and get this done before more people die. It isn't about anyone's ego. It's about getting those opportunists off the street and in prison where they belong."

Bleu turned to Royce. "I guess we're on board."

"Good, then I'll make the call. We need to meet up in person with the sheriff's office and the state police. I'll see what I can do about getting people from both departments here first thing in the morning. I think we should all be in attendance."

"Agreed," Bleu said. "Now what do we need to follow up on tonight?"

It was after six o'clock when those of us on the day shift clocked out. Before we left, I'd passed on the information we'd gotten about Donny and said that Prentice and Bloom should pay him a visit. After I plugged his name into the system, it appeared that he had been arrested twice for disturbing the peace and aggravated assault on a woman and spent six months in Hinesville at the Liberty County Jail.

"Interview him and find out where he was and what he was doing when Val and LeAnn went missing. Make sure his alibi is legit."

"Not a problem," Prentice said. "We'll take care of that right away."

Chapter 35

Rue and I walked to our cars together. "You sure you're good with teaming up?"

He shrugged. "It isn't about us. It's about the innocent victims."

I agreed completely. "I just hope once the information about seeing the trooper along the highway hits the airwaves, the phone lines at the state police headquarters light up like Christmas trees."

Rue sighed. "You know what we need right now, besides food?"

I chuckled. "What's that?"

"A stiff drink, and I can't think of anything better than a glass of Scotch."

"Really?"

"Yep. That and a greasy double cheeseburger and spicy fries."

"Humph. The place that serves the best cheeseburgers and spicy fries is Sparky's. Their burgers even come with extra grease."

"Yum. Wanna have supper there?"

"Sure. Why not? I'll be right behind you."

"Nope. We both know what happened last time you were right behind me. Tonight, you're taking the lead."

We found parking a half block from Sparky's. It was Thursday night and still somewhat early for the tourist crowds to hit the bars. They usually found restaurants first, enjoyed supper, and frequented the bars afterward, yet the real action didn't begin until Friday night.

Tomorrow night would be a week since Valerie had gone missing at bar-closing time. To catch a killer of three in one week would be remarkable, but detectives usually felt even that length of time wasn't quick enough. If the perp had been caught sooner, other innocent people wouldn't have died. Most police officers felt that way no matter what the case or where it happened, but like everyone else, we were only human and did the best we could.

Rue and I walked in and found an empty bar table. For eating, that was more desirable than sitting at the bar. Plus having a conversation was easier when facing each other.

A waitress quickly approached us and took our food and drink order. Besides the Scotch, we both ordered large sodas to drink with our meal.

After she took our orders, I noticed the waitress talking to T. J. I assumed he'd asked her if we wanted our Scotch on the rocks or neat. We'd said neat, but maybe she didn't know what that meant. T. J. walked over and confirmed our orders.

"Still working, huh?" I asked.

"Yeah, until eight. Better to get out of here before the crowd starts up, but of course, weekends are always the busiest. So neat on the Scotch?"

"Yep," Rue said. "We did say that."

"Yeah, but she's new. Just making sure."

"No problem," I said.

T. J. began to walk away but turned back. "You guys talk to Donny yet?"

"Night shift is taking care of it."

With a nod, he returned to the bar.

Rue and I discussed the case while we enjoyed a delicious supper and an even better Scotch. With all of our departments working together and sharing information, we were sure that the killer's enterprise would soon be nipped in the bud.

We paid the check, said good night to the staff and customers we recognized, and walked to our cars.

"I'm looking forward to tomorrow morning, and I sure hope Royce was able to get something set up," I said.

Rue and I parted ways, each headed home and likely thinking about the case until we fell asleep. At least, I knew I would.

Chapter 36

Chase's idea was not only risky but also one they hadn't attempted before. He'd suggested they stake out the inns and cottages on Tybee Island, where many tourists stayed. They would look for a woman walking alone to or from her vehicle then ask for directions while holding out a brochure as a prop. The plan was similar to when they'd snatched Valerie except for the fact that it wasn't two a.m. They would have to be near the van, grab her before she yelled out, and peel off before anyone saw, heard, or suspected anything.

The plan was daring, and Chase usually erred on the side of caution, not because he was afraid but because he wanted their enterprise to last at least another year before they took a break. He was sure they could pull it off, though, and since Teddy was at work anyway, he decided to check out the area himself.

It was a half-hour drive, but Chase had plenty of time and nothing better to do. Once on the island, he drove the popular route, US Highway 80 to Butler Avenue. He checked out the smaller, less-populated inns and cottages and found two that would be perfect if he and Teddy were lucky enough to see a woman alone. The parking lots held about ten cars at most, and they were somewhat private locations with large palms and potted plants to ensure privacy for their guests. They would return later, look for a woman alone or, worst case, a man they could handle, and take it from there. After that? Move on to other cities, take care of business, and return to Savannah on the weekends for rest and relaxation.

With the plan firmly planted and sure to be a success, Chase returned home and waited for Teddy. It wasn't long before he heard a car pull into the driveway then the sound of a key turned in the front door. His brother was home, and Chase was excited to share his news.

"What's up, buddy?" Teddy asked.

"We're going on a run."

"We are?"

"Yep, to Tybee Island. I've already scoped it out. The person we nab will likely be a tourist, so that's a plus, and we can dump the remains out in the marsh again."

"But that first girl was found."

"So what? The second woman was found, too, but as long as we stay under the radar, it doesn't matter. We'll be right in the marsh area anyway, so we'll look for an even more remote spot. I've already talked to Mr. Harris, and he's agreed to meet us halfway once we let him know we're on our way."

Teddy shrugged. "If you say so."

Chase was ready to head out. It would be a long night no matter what, and the sooner they left the better. Because Tybee Island was a tourist hot spot, most women would either be part of a group or with a man. Still, arriving in the area around nine o'clock seemed safe. Tourists were out and about, and finding a woman alone who might be meeting up with friends wasn't out of the question.

"We could wait until bar time like we did last week and grab someone right here in Savannah," Teddy said.

"Nah, I've already checked it out. The cops are patrolling the bar area too closely. We have to go somewhere that they haven't thought of. Come on. It'll be fine."

They reached the Cozy Inn at ten after nine. Chase turned in and shifted into Park at the end of the lot.

"We've got to scope out the situation for a few minutes before I decide how we're going to do this."

"I don't know, man. It looks kind of dead."

Chase laughed at the irony. "That's exactly how it's supposed to look, at least once we have someone in the back of the van. I grabbed some brochures earlier to use as props. We'll run the stupid-guy routine and say that we can't find the Coastal Cove Cottages. Of course, anyone who's been here for at least a day knows where they're at. You can't miss them two blocks up the street."

Teddy nodded, but his expression said he was less confident than his brother.

"What's wrong? You were a tough guy with the trooper the other day, and then cutting him up and handing his organs to Mr. Harris on a silver platter was brilliant. Don't turn into a chickenshit now. Remember that luxury boat we're going to buy?"

"Yeah, yeah, I'm fine. Guess this is a little out of my comfort zone. I mean, the area in general is pretty populated. What if she screams and someone hears her?"

"I'll be in charge. You just follow my lead." Chase looked through the side mirror as a car turned in and parked. "Here comes someone. Let's see who gets out."

Chase lowered his window, and they watched as three women who looked young, fearless, and clueless climbed out. Chase cocked his head and listened to their conversation as they emptied the trunk of what looked to be beach bags. One said something about cleaning up then hitting the bars. The others laughed and said they'd already drunk a twelve-pack of beer.

Chase grinned from ear to ear. "That's perfect. They're half in the bag already."

Teddy's sigh said he wasn't so sure. "What good are they to us? We can't grab all three."

"Let's just see where they go. If we have to move on, we will. Be patient, little brother. It'll all work out in the end."

They watched as the ladies walked toward a unit at the end of the building, which was partially blocked by potted plants. Once they were out of sight, Chase pulled in and parked next to the vehicle the women had just left. No sooner had he killed the lights than one of the girls yelled out that she'd left her cell phone in the car and would be right back.

"Hurry, jump out of the van! We'll come up from behind when she's preoccupied at the car. Call out to her, and as soon as she turns, punch her in the face. I'll get the van door, you secure her, and we'll be out of here in under a minute. There's no time to think, so move!" Chase followed Teddy out the side door. They waited in the shadows as the young lady approached the car she had just gotten out of and fumbled with the key fob until the lights flashed and a beep sounded. She grabbed the passenger-side door handle and pulled it open.

Chase gave Teddy a nudge to go then pointed at the van. He whispered, "Now!"

Not making a sound and coming up from behind,

Teddy called out to her. He was within striking distance when she turned.

"Damn, dude, you scared the shit out—"

Teddy's fist was already cocked when she turned around, and a sucker punch to the face stunned her long enough for him to load her into the van.

After slamming the sliding door, Chase jumped into the driver's seat, backed up, and spun around. He barreled onto the street in hopes of making a quick exit out of town.

"Hey, I can't secure her by myself. The bitch is coming around."

"Punch her again!" Chase said. "We need to get out of town. Shit! Now I have to wait for this line of cars to pass before I can turn."

Just then, the woman kicked Teddy with all her might. He flew backward and cracked his head against the rear of the van.

"Shit!" Chase slammed the shifter into Park as the girl reached for the door handle. He leapt over the seat and grabbed her by the hair just as she opened the door. She screamed, and he yanked her in but not before a bystander waiting at the crosswalk caught a glimpse of her.

Chase yelled out to Teddy. "Damn it, help me! I've got to get us out of here."

Teddy grabbed the woman and pinned her to the floor as Chase returned to the driver's seat, gunned the van, and turned left onto Highway 80 heading north. There was still a mile to go before he would be out of the tourist trap area, then he could hit the gas and get distance between them and that Tybee Island tourist who might have called 911.

"Is she down?" Chase jerked his head to the right and looked over the seat.

"Yeah, I think I knocked her out this time. Son of a bitch, she caught me off guard."

"Yeah, and that might have been our undoing. A guy on the sidewalk saw her when she tried to get out, and that means he saw the van too."

"Now what?"

"Now we get the hell out of here, go home, hopefully without incident, and take care of her there. We'll have to regroup, use your car to deliver the organs, and then decide on our next move."

After arriving home a half hour later, Chase backed the van into the garage, got out, and slid the side door open. "Geez, Teddy, her face looks like hamburger."

Teddy shrugged as he climbed out and stood next to Chase. "I had no choice, and nobody cares about her face anyway."

Chase let out a groan and lowered the overhead. "Okay, I'll yank her out, and you lay a tarp on the floor."

Chapter 37

On Friday morning, I woke with thoughts of Valerie. The what-ifs started playing in my head. What if she had changed her mind and hadn't gone out that night? What if the girls had bypassed Sparky's and called it a night earlier? What if Valerie hadn't parked so far away or walked to her car alone? None of those questions would ever be answered. It was too late, and nobody could press the rewind button and take back that night. All we could do was hope that the joint effort between law enforcement agencies would prove successful. With any luck, we would find the killers before the what-ifs filled my mind again—new ones of LeAnn and the night she'd died.

I was excited to get to work, and a text from Royce late last night had confirmed that the meeting that morning was good to go. Several representatives from the state police, the Bulloch County Sheriff's Office, and the Statesboro PD would be sitting in on our group meeting.

The Bulloch County medical examiner, along with

Tapper, would be part of that meeting, too, and side by side, they would compare the manner of death and autopsy reports.

After a quick breakfast of a granola bar, a banana, and coffee, I headed out. I wanted to be ready for that meeting, which Royce said would begin at eight o'clock sharp in the downstairs conference room, which was far larger than ours on the second floor.

Rue called my cell phone as I drove. Because my rental was a brand-new model, I spoke to Devon through my phone synced into the infotainment center.

"Hey, what's up?" I asked.

"Just wondering if you got a text from Royce last night to get to work on time."

"Of course, and when am I ever not on time?"

"Good point. Anyway, it'll be downstairs."

I looked both ways at the stop sign then continued on. "Already know that too. Are you there?"

"Nope, just leaving home."

"Then it looks like I'll get there before you."

"Darn."

I chuckled. "Is that all you wanted?"

"No. Grab me a coffee so I don't have to look like a jerk by being the last one entering the conference room."

"Yeah, yeah." I hung up and smiled.

My entire life, I'd wished I had a brother, yet my partner, Devon, was the brother I'd never had, and I would do anything for him. He would do the same for me, and my entire family and I were grateful.

After parking, I walked upstairs to my office and grabbed two notepads and two pens. I was sure if Rue didn't have time to get his own coffee, he would have even less time to grab a pad of paper and a pen. I continued down the hall to the cafeteria and bought two coffees.

Now how the hell am I going to carry everything?

Grumbling, I pocketed the pens, jammed the notepads in my waistband, and carried the coffees down two flights of stairs. Rue had just opened the outer door as I was passing.

"Good timing. Here, take your stuff."

"Thanks, partner."

We headed into the conference room, where Royce, Bleu, and two strangers were already seated. At least ten other people were expected to show up. As we waited, Royce made the introductions. Both men, Ken Jarrett and Dan Westfall, were from the state police. After handshakes, Rue and I sat down as more people entered the room.

Bentley, Lawrence, Bloom, and Prentice came in next, I assumed because they were local and lived within ten minutes of the precinct. We were still waiting on representatives from the Bulloch County Sheriff's Office and the Statesboro Police Department.

We made small talk until everyone showed up at a quarter after eight with apologies about traffic on the highway.

I smiled at the thought of them having used their sirens to arrive sooner, but since getting to a meeting wasn't considered an emergency, I imagined they knew better.

After the introductions were made, Ken Jarrett began the meeting simply because he ranked highest of everyone in attendance.

"First and foremost, I want to thank Sergeant Royce for bringing up the idea of contacting the news stations and airing a plea for help from the public. With that plea ongoing, I'm happy to say we've been getting leads. Once we have at least fifty descriptions of the vehicle that was pulled over by the trooper and we compare descriptions, it'll be easy to see if there's a vehicle that is consistently mentioned. If there's twenty black trucks described and all the others are random vehicles, then I'd likely put my money on the vehicle being the black truck. See where I'm going with this?"

Everyone nodded.

"Good. We'll give it a couple of days, and by then, we should have a good representation."

I couldn't believe he said "a couple of days." We were already a couple of days *behind* in finding and arresting the culprit, but I remained quiet.

Ken went on to agree with Royce that we needed to share all incidents related to the murders and organ removal of the victims so far, plus any new findings. That much, I completely agreed with. Information was king, and every ounce of it we could gather would help. I wrote as he talked.

We had to compare the list of family and friends of the trooper to similar lists from our Chatham County victims. Our counties also needed to compare statements that had been called in about suspicious characters or vehicles, and we needed to share knowledge of past criminals throughout Georgia who had behaved in a way that could advance to murder and organ removal. Any for-profit crime could progress to selling body parts if the perp was desperate or savvy enough to pull it off. We also had the buyers to deal with, and that information would have to be gathered from the national criminal database. Royce might be more open to that idea now that other agencies were involved and he wouldn't be stretching his detectives too thin.

"Have you gotten any leads at all in the trooper's murder?" Royce asked.

Bill Randall from the sheriff's office responded. "The location where the trooper's car was found was very remote. There weren't any houses in the area and definitely none down that deserted road. All we have to hope for is enough people calling in who saw the same vehicle pulled over by the trooper. Until that happens, we don't have fingerprints, video footage, or even tire tracks to make plaster casts from. We didn't find a speck of evidence dropped or left behind, and we searched the area thoroughly."

Royce turned to Ken. "So, are the state police going to handle the responsibility of checking out previous organ buyers, if they're incarcerated, and if not, learning what they're up to now? I'd think you have more resources than we do."

Ken took notes then looked up. "We have plenty of individuals who can take care of that task."

Royce let out a long sigh. "We'll need to exchange phone numbers, work and cell, email addresses, and update each other with all news that's related to these murders. This investigation is moving far too slowly for my liking, but I guess that's because tonight will be the one-week anniversary of when Valerie went missing. Sunday morning will be a week since her hollowed-out body was found."

Dan Westfall looked around the table at each face. "Detectives? We need feedback since you're likely going to be the feet on the ground."

I spoke up. "We retraced our steps and interviewed everyone again in the Valerie Dawson case. The footage was given a second look too. Nothing new other than an additional name came up."

Dan frowned. "And?"

Prentice took his turn. "And it was a dead end. Just a creepy guy who served time behind bars but had solid alibis for both nights in question."

Royce pointed his chin at Dan. "So the trooper's wife has been checked out? Kids, neighbors, the whole gamut? No mysterious bank account withdrawals or life insurance policies recently taken out on the trooper, that sort of thing?"

"Nope. Nothing fishy, and the friends and family are clean and alibied."

"Okay, then we're all on the same page. We're starting from scratch with nothing to work with until calls come in about the last vehicle the trooper pulled over."

Ken agreed. "It looks that way. We'll get started on every organ buyer who has been arrested in the US over the last five years."

With a grunt, Royce pushed back his chair and stretched. "Then I guess our part is done. Tapper, you and Dr. Kingman want to take it from here?"

Tapper nodded and began. "I'm quite positive we wouldn't be sitting here today if it wasn't for Dr. Kingman. The fact that he shared the autopsy reports with other county coroners was huge. Now, as a joint effort, these killings might end. In comparing the reports, the similarities between victims is uncanny, down to the precise way the killer removed the organs. We have no doubt that the killers are the same in all three murders."

My mind was going in circles. "According to the autopsy reports, each victim had been dead for around ten hours when found. That gave the killers plenty of time to commit the murder, remove the organs, dump the body, and then drive to wherever they were selling the organs. It also seemed that even though the perps tried to hide the remains, doing so was almost an afterthought. Their main focus was getting the organs to the buyer within a certain amount of time."

Dr. Kingman cleared his throat then spoke up. "The kidneys have the longest shelf life, but in order to streamline their efforts, I'm sure they sold all the organs to the same buyer. That way, they're paid and can start the hunt all over again with a clean slate."

"So, they were heading north out of Savannah when they were pulled over just outside Statesboro," Royce said.

The deputy confirmed that. "Actually, just north of Statesboro on US Highway 80, about halfway between Statesboro and Akins Mill."

I took my turn. "I wonder where they were going. The closest big city in a northerly direction is Augusta. They have multiple hospitals and a regional airport too." I noticed Ken taking notes. "Were they making a delivery and happened to get pulled over? Did they look at the trooper as a bonus opportunity, another payday? All sick ideas, but in the minds of sick people, it seems acceptable. The reward is worth the risk."

"And the trooper likely bled out from a stab to the carotid artery," Dr. Kingman said.

"Good point," Royce said, "and on a busy highway, where does a trooper go when he approaches a vehicle?"

Rue huffed. "To the passenger-side window, and it was his right carotid artery that was severed."

"Meaning there was definitely someone in the passenger seat. My question is, how did they put the trooper in their car and drive his away without a single passerby noticing?" I asked.

Ken took over. "Not in the trunk unless they timed it perfectly when there wasn't traffic coming."

I looked at the deputies. "They needed a workstation of sorts, and according to what you said, there wasn't a single clue, drop of blood, or speck of evidence at the scene."

Rue locked eyes on me. "It had to be a van."

Royce pressed his temples with his palms. "Son of a bitch."

Chapter 38

With the state police, the Bulloch County Sheriff's Office, the Statesboro Police Department, and our own PD on board, I saw a certain amount of confidence between everyone as the meeting came to an end. Our heads were lifted a little higher, our shoulders weren't slumped, and our backs were straight. We had a clear vision and a path to follow, and we would all work together as a cohesive unit to bring the killers to justice.

With handshakes and thanks, we parted ways and promised to update each agency at least twice a day.

We needed to have a sit-down with Royce again about the van situation. We were sure Jacob wasn't involved, so it had to be two other men who also had a van—for convenience if nothing else. As disgusting as it sounded, it was their organ-removal workstation on wheels.

We joined Royce in his office, where we dropped down onto the guest chairs.

"So, what is our task going to be?" I asked. "We've got four detectives who are sitting on their hands and waiting for someone in a neighboring county to call someone else in another county to report a vehicle pulled over along the highway two days ago. I'd be lucky to remember what I saw forty-eight hours ago as I'm speeding down the highway at seventy miles an hour, and I'm a cop."

Royce opened his desk drawer, pulled out a bottle of ibuprofen, and shook three tablets into his hand. He tossed them into his mouth and washed them down with cold coffee.

"Nine thirty and I already have a splitting headache." He eyeballed me for a second and then said to pursue that van theory again.

Rue and I headed to our office. We had a lot of digging to do. I started by calling down to Missing Persons first. We needed to know if anyone else in our jurisdiction had been reported missing in the last two days. I was told that no one had been, but the PD in Tybee Island had a missing person report filed on an out-of-town woman who'd vanished without a trace just last night. The friends she was vacationing with went into the Tybee Island police station that morning and filed the report.

"Can you email that to me, Miranda? That'd be a lot easier than trying to write down everything."

Miranda said she would. I thanked her, hung up, and dialed the Tybee Island PD. The missing woman was still unaccounted for. The officer I spoke with mentioned a strange call that came in last night. The caller wasn't sure whether he'd witnessed people acting out or if something serious was going on. He said a woman was yelling and trying to get out of a vehicle but was jerked back in. He thought it could possibly be a boyfriend-and-girlfriend argument.

I asked for that report, too, and not five minutes later, both had landed in my email.

"Rue, come look at these reports with me."

Devon rolled his chair over and, with his arm propped on my desk, held his chin up with his hand. "This one is the Tybee Island missing tourist report?"

"Yep. After spending the day at the beach then finally returning to the room at the Cozy Inn, Gina Casey remembered leaving her cell phone in the car. She went out to retrieve it and never returned to the room she shared with her two friends. The report says they were going to hit the bars after showering. One friend was taking her shower while the other dozed off on the bed, and neither realized Gina hadn't returned to the room for a good half hour. They went out to the car, saw her cell phone was still inside, and spent the night driving around looking for her."

"Why in the hell wouldn't they contact the police right away?"

"Because they're dumb kids and their brains haven't matured yet. That's why. They wasted the entire night looking for her instead of thinking foul play might be involved."

I opened the next report, which was the one about the yelling female in the car. According to that report, the caller said the woman was holding open the sliding side door of a van and screaming, then a man yanked her back inside and the van sped away.

My eyes bulged as I stared at the screen. "Did I just read that right?"

"Yep, you sure did, and we need to speak with that caller as soon as possible."

I dialed the Tybee Island Police Department back and said it was imperative that we speak to the person who had made that 911 call. I was transferred to the sergeant in charge, who said the call came into Dispatch and the nearest patrol officer in the area took the report from the man at the scene.

"But his personal information was collected, too, correct?"

"Yes, Detective Cannon, it was, but the guy is also a tourist. He isn't from Georgia, so I don't know how much a copy of his driver's license is going to help you."

"It'll have to be good enough unless he told the officer where he's staying."

"That wasn't included with his statement."

"Okay, then I'll need someone to send a copy of the license to my email address. It sounds like that incident the caller saw last night and the missing tourist this morning could be connected, especially with the mention of a van. They could be part of the ongoing investigation we've been working on for a week."

"I'll have our records clerk send you the man's contact information right away. All I need is your email address again."

After giving it to him, I was told that I'd have the information within minutes. I thanked him and hung up.

"Now we wait."

Rue grabbed the receiver from his desk phone. "I'll call Royce and tell him what we just found out."

I listened to Rue's side of the conversation and, through the phone lines, heard Royce's cursing. Devon hung up.

"He isn't happy."

"Yeah, I bet. But for now, we have to find out more about that missing girl. We need to speak to those friends of hers, too, but first, it's imperative we track down the man who called 911." Minutes later, the email came in with a copy of the caller's driver's license. "Okay, the guy is from Jacksonville, Florida. Type his name into the people search database and see if we get an address match and phone number."

I waited as Rue tapped the computer keys.

"Got it. Here's the phone number."

I dialed it, and a man's voice answered. I asked if he was Adam Zimmer, and he said he was. I told him who I was and what I needed to know. I also asked him to be as detailed as possible. I wanted to know everything he'd seen—which direction the van was going, a description of the vehicle and the woman screaming, and the man who pulled her back into the van.

"Um, it happened so fast. I mean, it wasn't like I could rewind what I saw and memorize every detail. Literally from the minute the woman screamed for help until the van was out of sight took about five seconds. Plus, last night, I told the officer everything that was fresh in my mind."

"I understand that, but what you saw could be connected to a murder case we're working on here in Savannah. I can't go into detail about that, but that's the reason facts are so important. Even if you told the officer what went down, did you describe the van to him? Did you get a plate number, notice if there was damage to the vehicle or possibly window or bumper stickers to help identify it?"

"Wow. I don't remember any of that other than the van was light colored. Could have been white, silver, light gray, tan, so I'm not sure. My eyes were fixated on the girl."

"Okay, what did she look like, and what was she wearing?"

"Damn. She had chin-length brown hair, and it

looked like she wore some kind of flowery beach coverup. She was young—under thirty for sure—but that's it. I was standing on the sidewalk about forty feet from the van as it barreled through the intersection."

"In what direction?"

"Sir, I'm not from Tybee Island, so I don't know my directions from street corners."

"The police report says you were on the corner of Second Avenue and Highway 80."

"That's right."

"So which way did the van go?"

"It passed me on Highway 80, I guess."

"So toward the water or heading inland?"

"Inland."

"Okay, great. Where are you staying, Adam, and how long will you be on the island?"

"I'm actually heading back to Jacksonville this afternoon."

"All right. Thanks for your help, and there could be the chance that I'll call again. Have a safe trip home." I hung up and dialed the missing persons department at the Tybee Island PD. We needed phone numbers for the two women who'd filed the report that morning, and I also wanted to find out if they had mentioned where they were staying. What had been forwarded to us was only the file on the missing woman but nothing about the people who'd filed the report. I was connected to the department and transferred to the officer who took the report.

"Officer Denton here."

"Officer Denton, this is Detective Cannon in Savannah. I understand you took a missing person report this morning from two young ladies."

"Yes, their friend went missing last night." I heard

what sounded like a frustrated sigh through the phone lines. "If only they would have come in right when it happened. Patrol could have been out looking for her."

"You took down the personal information from those ladies, correct?"

"Yes, of course. We can't have people playing pranks and making false claims, so we take down their personal information right away."

"Good. I'll need you to email that to me as soon as possible. I believe the missing girl could be a victim in a case we're investigating."

"You bet. I'll send it over right away."

After giving him my email address, I waited again. That time when the information came through, it included copies of both driver's licenses and the phone numbers. That would speed up the process, and I dialed the first number immediately.

The voice on the other end sounded shaky as if she had been crying. I looked at the copy of her driver's license and saw a photo of the young lady I was talking to.

"Is this Ellen Barnes?"

"It is. Who's this?"

"I'm a detective from Savannah. We learned of Gina's disappearance this morning and wondered if anything new has come up."

"No, but the Tybee Island police are handling it."

"Sort of. Can you describe Gina for me?"

Ellen began to cry. "She has medium-length brown hair, and she's skinny. She's twenty-two and missing. Her parents are going to shit!"

Ellen's voice went from sad and shaky to a high-pitched, frantic shrill. I heard someone talking in the background, then they got on the line.

"I'm Tory Hughes. We can't track Gina, text her, or call her because her phone and purse are here. She just disappeared with no way to contact anyone and no money."

"Tory, can you stay calm for me?"

"I guess."

"Good. What did you girls do yesterday?"

"We were at the beach all day."

"Did any guys make unwanted advances at you or come on too strong?"

"No, we didn't talk to any guys except the bartender at the beach bar."

"So I understand when you ladies got back to your room, you had plans to go out to the bars that night."

"Yes. Gina was going to check out the cool places on her phone while I showered. That's when she realized she left her phone in the car. She went out to get it, and that was the last time we had any contact with her."

"Was there a reason you waited until morning to file the report?"

"We were scared. We didn't want her parents to worry, and we figured we'd find her hanging out with some guy."

I heard her voice catch in her throat.

"But we never did."

"Can you take a picture of her license and email it to me?"

"Yes."

"And how long are you girls going to be in Tybee Island?"

"Until tomorrow. We're flying out of Savannah at five o'clock."

"To?"

"Home. We live in Richmond, Virginia."

"Okay, can you girls just hang tight? My partner and I can be there in a half hour. We'd like to go over everything with you again and then check out Gina's belongings."

"Yes, we'll stay here. We're at the Cozy Inn, room seven at the end of the building."

"Great. We'll be there soon."

I opened my email and snapped a picture of Gina's driver's license. After I shut down my laptop, Rue and I passed Royce's office and told him we were heading out.

"Find out something so I can pass it on to the others," Royce said.

I gave him a head tip. "That's the plan."

Chapter 39

It was nearly noon by the time we reached the Cozy Inn. I parked, and we followed the numbered doors to room seven. I gave the door a knuckle rap, and a cute blonde who reminded me of a younger version of my sister Meg pulled open the door.

I nodded a hello and showed her my badge. "We're Detectives Cannon and Rue, and you are?"

"Tory." She looked around the small room. "Um—"

"We passed a picnic table when we were walking to your room. How about we sit there and talk, okay?" I asked.

She smiled. "Yeah, that would be good." She called out to Ellen, who said she would be right with us—she was brushing her teeth.

We stepped outside, and a mere thirty feet away was a vine-covered pergola surrounded by plants with a picnic table centered in the space. It was shady and private, a perfect spot to have a confidential conversation. I set my notepad, pen, and phone on the table.

Seconds later, Ellen joined us. We introduced ourselves, and she took a seat next to Tory.

"Okay, we're going to run some questions by you about Gina and then take a look at her phone. Sound good?"

They both nodded, and Tory spoke up before we began. "Why are the Savannah police involved when Gina disappeared here and we've already told the Tybee Island police everything we know?"

"Because the Tybee Island police are looking for Gina on the island. She's considered missing and nothing more as far as they know."

"As far as they know?" Ellen asked. "What does that mean?"

"We believe Gina has been abducted. A 911 call came in last night a few blocks from here about a young woman seen trying to get out of a van, but a man yanked her back in. Do you remember what Gina was wearing when she walked out to the car?"

"Yeah," Tory said. "We'd only been back a few minutes, so she still had on her swimsuit and a cover-up over it."

"Can you describe the cover-up?" Rue asked.

"It has sunflowers on it."

I glanced at Rue. The woman Adam had seen in the van was looking more and more like Gina, and my gut said she was likely already dead. We needed a good view of that van and an accurate color of it. A thought came to mind, and I rose from the table.

"Go ahead with the interview, Devon. I'm going to look around for a few minutes."

"No problem."

I headed for the parking lot where the rental car was but backtracked to the picnic table. "Is your rental parked in the same place it was when you came back from the beach?"

Ellen answered. "Yes, it's in the same spot."

"Okay, thanks." I walked through the pea-gravel lot and scanned the ground around the car, but nothing stood out. I looked up at the palm trees and the corners of the building—no cameras. Since the parking lot was relatively small, the street wasn't far away. I walked out to the sidewalk and looked in every direction for a camera. "Bingo."

Across the street, a bank was near the intersection. It had a corner-mounted camera at the roofline, and I needed to view their footage from last night. I called Rue's cell and explained where I was going. The chance of seeing that van pass by was great. I asked Rue to find out what time the girls returned to the inn from the beach. I heard them talking, then Rue came back on the line.

"The girls said they were back a little after nine. They went to a fast-food restaurant right after the beach, had burgers, and then came here."

"Okay, I'll be across the street at the bank when you're done there." I hung up, looked both ways before stepping off the curb, then crossed the street.

After entering the bank, I explained to the manager who I was and what I needed. She was more than happy to oblige and said their cameras recorded twenty-four hours a day. From the location where the outside camera was mounted, it would catch the intersection in all direc-tions. The van had to have passed, and hopefully, some-thing about it would stand out. If I was lucky, I might get a plate number too.

I joined the manager in the bank's security office, and even though there were probably other street-facing cameras in the neighborhood, the bank would likely have the best-quality security system of them all.

The manager, Jean Foss, set the time frame I needed then hit Play.

"Sorry, but I'll have to stay in here with you, Detective Cannon. Bank security, you know."

"Perfectly understandable, and this shouldn't take too long since the time frame isn't in question."

I knew when the van was at the Cozy Inn, and I knew what time Adam had made the 911 call. There wasn't any guesswork involved. I had less than a ten-minute window that the van could pass through the video frame.

I watched the screen as cars came and went. They stopped at the red lights or continued through the green ones.

"There!" I couldn't help yelling and had forgotten the manager was sitting only five feet away. I hit Pause, apologized for startling her, then regrouped. My pen and notepad sat on the desk next to me. I backed up the footage then pressed Play again. With my finger hovering over the pause key, I stared at the screen until the front of the van came into the frame. I paused the footage, zoomed in as far as I could, and took note of every square inch I was looking at. The driver's-side mirror was intact, just like the one that passed the mall camera after LeAnn was abducted. The van was definitely white, which I could tell thanks to the color camera system. I wrote down that the windows were tinted, which made the driver impossible to see. I looked at the front rims then forwarded the footage slightly. I reached the center of the van and paused the video again. Nothing in that area was remarkable, and there weren't any side windows on the panel van.

I moved to the rear. The rims were the same as the front ones, the gas tank was on that side, and a mud flap was behind the rear driver's-side tire. Other than that, the vehicle was pretty standard. It had no advertising decals or stickers of any kind. Now I needed it to turn right. It would be the only way to see anything from the rear, including a plate number.

"Come on. Turn right."

Turning left or going straight would give me nothing. I wanted to see if there were rear doors, and if there were, I was looking at the wrong van. I pressed Play and watched as the van approached the intersection at the green light and turned left. I cursed under my breath. What I saw was all I would get unless we chased down every camera facing Highway 80. We'd also have to find cameras on the northeast side of the street to see if the van had a sliding side door, yet chasing down images of the van seemed too time-consuming. From the timeline, I was certain that the van on the bank's security camera was the one Gina was in, and I couldn't even let myself think of what had happened inside or beyond that point.

With my phone, I snapped a half-dozen screenshots of the van, thanked Jean, and headed to the inn.

The interviews were over, and Rue sat at the picnic table while looking through Gina's phone. He had written down all the names and numbers that were relevant according to Ellen and Tory. They'd also told Devon that Gina had no enemies whatsoever and worked part-time at a grocery store in Richmond. Devon had already given the girls his card, and after returning Gina's phone, we thanked them and left.

We climbed into the cruiser, and Rue said he had called the Tybee Island PD to find out if Gina's parents had been notified about their missing daughter. He was told they had and that the Tybee Island PD would handle all communication with Mr. and Mrs. Casey.

Rue cracked his neck from side to side before pulling his seat belt across his chest. "So, what did you find out?"

"I saw the van. I mean, I saw *a* van, but I know it was the right one. It turned back toward Savannah on Highway 80, which means I only saw the driver's side."

"So could you make out what the driver looked like?"

I groaned. "Hell no. The windows were tinted."

Rue cursed. "Are we ever going to catch a break? Meanwhile, Gina's life is hanging in the balance."

I slapped the steering wheel in frustration. "All we can do is see if Royce actually put out that BOLO on the van, and if he didn't, it needs to be done immediately. Every white van that Patrol comes across in Savannah has to be pulled over and the occupants need to be questioned. We don't have the luxury of time anymore, and neither does Gina Casey."

Chapter 40

Rue called Royce and set the phone to Speaker as I drove. He asked about the BOLO, and Royce said he hadn't talked to Sergeant Hatch about it yet. First, he wanted to know what we had found out.

I couldn't tell Royce that he had made a mistake by not putting the BOLO in place yesterday, but he had, and it was a mistake that might have cost Gina her life.

I spoke up. "Boss, it's Mitch. I saw the van on a bank's security camera, and it's definitely white and resembles the one that sped out of the mall parking lot. I didn't get a look at the passenger side or see anything as far as plate number, but I think that BOLO needs to go out anyway. If those killers are shaken up now because Adam witnessed Gina trying to escape, they might flee Savannah and be gone for good."

Expletives poured out of Royce's mouth before he caught his breath and returned his focus to the phone call. "Okay, I'll get it out now and go countywide with it. Anyone driving a white van in Chatham County who is spotted by a patrol officer or a deputy will be pulled over and questioned." He hung up without asking anything else.

I shook my head and couldn't say the words, but from the look Rue gave me, he was likely thinking the same thing.

"Do you think Gina is still alive?"

I did my own share of cursing. "Honestly? No. Especially if the killers got spooked. They probably ended her life last night, sold her body parts already, and disposed of her remains before they went to bed. Chances are, they're going to either get rid of that van, have it painted, or get the hell out of Dodge."

"Then does it even matter now if a witness calls in that they saw a vehicle pulled over by the trooper late that afternoon?"

"It matters in the sense that it'll solidify what we already suspected days ago—that somebody in a white van is kidnapping, killing, and selling the body parts of young ladies."

"And a state trooper too."

We arrived at the precinct and checked in with Royce. He said that he had just gotten word from the state police that six callers confirmed a white van as a vehicle they'd seen pulled over by a trooper. Nobody saw a sliding side door, though, since the vehicle was northbound and the passenger side was along the ditch.

"Well, that's all the proof I need, and that's the route you would take to Augusta," I said.

Royce raised his brows. "True enough. I need to call Ken back and see if any organ sellers came out of Augusta or neighboring areas. We also need to know how long the sentences were that those people served and if they're still incarcerated. If they are, then there's likely a group of newcomers who have taken their place." My frown caught Royce's attention. "Something on your mind, Cannon?"

"Yeah, there is. An idea, actually. We've been spinning our wheels and going to locations that the van has been to after the fact."

"Right. And?"

"And how about we look for it proactively?"

"The countywide BOLO is in place already."

"Not what I mean. We looked through the camera footage of every store along Valerie's walk back to her car. How about we do that again except widen the search?"

Now Royce frowned. "I'm not following."

"Maybe the killers scouted out the bar district ahead of time, and maybe they went back afterward to see if there was a larger police presence in the area. At least now we know what we're looking for. If we catch that van on video days before or days after Valerie was abducted, we might get a plate number or even see the occupants get in or out of the vehicle. They would never think about their images or a sighting of the van being on a number of cameras downtown in the historic district or the bar and restaurant area. Some of those cameras might record for a week or more before they start over."

Rue nodded as I talked. He looked to be in agreement. "I like it," he said.

"Yeah, I do too. Okay, get on it and have Bentley and Lawrence pitch in," Royce said.

We updated Curt and John before we left, and they agreed to go through the footage we already had for the third time. Rue and I would return to Sparky's and a few other stores in that general area to put eyes on their footage recorded several days before and after Valerie went missing. That would be time-consuming, but we were looking for only one thing—a white van. Everything else, we would speed through.

Once we reached Sparky's, I parked along the curb, and we walked in. It was already late afternoon, and the bar seating was filling up. The noise level was high with the music louder than it usually was at noon. Rue and I made our way to the only vacant bar table. It hadn't been cleaned off yet, but I didn't intend to be there for more than a few minutes anyway. I just needed to get somebody's attention. I scanned the bar and didn't see T. J., so I assumed it was his day off.

Minutes later, Becky, a longtime waitress there, walked over carrying a tray. She apologized as she cleared the table and said something about being short-handed. T. J. had up and quit without the required two weeks' notice.

"Yeah, I'm kind of waitressing and bartending today. The supper crowd will be showing up soon and then…" She chuckled. "Well, you know how the weekends are around here. So, Detectives, what can I get you?"

"Not a problem," I said. "Actually, we came to speak with the manager."

"Sure. George is working today. I'll let him know you're here."

Several minutes later, George walked down the hallway. He waved us toward him, and Rue and I headed that way.

"What can I help you with, Detectives?"

"Sorry to bother you, George, but we need to look over your camera footage again," I said. "I know you're kind of in a lurch with T. J. quitting, but it's imperative we look at footage a few days before and after Valerie Dawson went missing."

"Yeah, damn employees. T. J. worked here for two years and quits without so much as a courtesy handshake. He texted me his resignation. Something about buying a boat with his brother and taking extended time away from the day-to-day workforce. Whatever the hell that means."

"Wow." I chuckled. "He must have gotten plenty of killer tips."

George shrugged. "Who knows? The employees keep their own tips and don't claim them as earnings. So, no leads yet?"

"We're making progress, although slow," Rue said. "By the way, do you know anyone who owns a white van?"

George rubbed his chin. "Nah, can't say that I do."

"Wishful thinking, I guess. Anyway, what we need is to look through your outdoor footage from the Wednesday before last to this past Tuesday. Is that possible?"

"Yep, not a problem. I'll set it up for you, then I have to go out front and help where it's needed."

"Thanks, George. Appreciate it."

George set up the footage and said it was ready to play. "You fellas want an appetizer or something to drink?"

I looked at Rue, knowing that we might be sitting there for a few hours. "How about some wings, fries, and a couple of sweet teas?"

"Coming right up."

I checked that the footage was set to begin a week ago Wednesday, and it was. "Okay, I'm going to play this at double speed. If it seems too fast, I'll slow it down, but just ignore everything that isn't a white van."

Rue gave me a head tip, and I pressed Play. Our eyes

darted from side to side as vehicles passed during the daylight hours and into the night. We hadn't glimpsed a single white van so far. We reached Friday night, the night Valerie was abducted after the bars closed. Since Lawrence and Bentley were reviewing that footage, we moved on to the next few days. Saturday proved useless, and I was sure Saturday night would too. The police presence in the area had doubled since it was the weekend and everyone liked to party, including tourists. Out-of-towners would be more difficult to track, especially if that person was a lone female.

I took a gulp of tea and excused myself to stretch and use the restroom. When I returned, Rue had already moved on to Sunday.

I checked the date and time stamp. "Damn it. I was hoping to get a glimpse of that van by now. Maybe I was completely off track with that suggestion."

Rue swiped the air. "Nah, don't sell yourself short. They're out there somewhere. Don't forget LeAnn was abducted Monday night, and that means they were still in Savannah."

We got through Sunday without seeing that elusive white van. A commercial van passed by and nearly gave me a heart attack until I saw the advertising for an air-conditioning service on the side. It also had double rear doors. My shoulders slumped, and my hopes had all but faded, but we pushed on and began with Monday.

I rubbed my eyes and refocused as we sped through the morning hours. I felt like a zombie and wondered how long we'd been staring at that computer screen. George had come in to check on us an hour earlier and filled our glasses with more iced tea. Car after car passed the outdoor camera that caught the immediate area at the front door and the sidewalk in both directions.

Rue yelled out, and I nearly fell off my chair.

"Did you see that?" His eyes bulged, and he hit Pause.

"Damn it, Rue. Are you trying to give me a heart attack? I don't know where you were looking. What did you see?"

"I caught what looked like a white van going down the side street. There was a car next to it, so I only saw the passenger-side rear panel."

"Back up the footage and play it at normal speed." I concentrated on the screen as Rue made the adjustments. "There. Stop!"

What we saw was just like Devon had said. We were looking at the rear quarter panel of a white van. Next to it, blocking most of our view, was a green sedan.

"What street is that?" I asked.

"Barnard, and there's a handful of county offices in that area. One of them has to have a camera so we can see where that van went."

"Okay." I snapped a picture of the video's time stamp, thanked George, and said we might be back, then we took off on foot. It wouldn't take but a minute to find outdoor cameras right around the corner.

Rue rushed ahead of me, as I still wasn't able to run. I walked fine as long as I had ibuprofen to curb the occasional pain, but running was still down the road. I told him to text his location as soon as he saw a camera.

The post office building took up the corner of State and Barnard, and I was certain I would hear from Rue any second. There had to be cameras on that three-story building. My phone vibrated in my pocket, and I fished it out.

"What do you have?"

"I'm inside the post office and just asked to speak with the postmaster."

"Okay, I'll be there in a second." I walked through the double doors, and Rue waited off to the side. "I hope we don't spend hours chasing down that van on every camera in the city."

"No kidding, right?" Rue pointed his chin at the door that was opening behind the counter. "That's got to be him."

A middle-aged man in business casual attire walked out and looked around. He wore a lanyard around his neck with glasses dangling from it. He locked eyes on us then pointed at the closed door with a plaque that read Postmaster attached to it. Rue and I walked that way and waited for him to allow us through.

After he opened the door, we introduced ourselves, explained what we needed, and were led to the back offices.

We learned his name was Lee Patterson and that he'd been the postmaster for nine years. After joining him in the room that held four computers, all recording live footage at the street level on each corner of the building, I told him we needed to see Monday's footage at a quarter till three. We were looking for a white van that passed by on Barnard heading north.

Mr. Patterson set up the camera that intersected with Barnard and State. "This should be the camera you're looking for. If that van passes, then we'll follow it with the camera on the north end of the building, but we'll lose it after a block."

"Okay, let's see what we have."

Rue and I pulled folding chairs closer, sat down, and stared at the monitor. We had about a minute or two before the van would come into view, but I wanted to make sure we didn't miss it. When we did see it, I also hoped to see the driver through the windshield.

Looking for a front plate as it came toward the camera wouldn't help. They weren't required in Georgia, but the next camera might catch the back plate. We could only hope. We were down to the wire. The van had to be the right one, the killers had to be inside, and we had to figure out who they were and apprehend them that day. Time wasn't on our side, and at the rate they were killing people, we had to get them off the street as soon as possible.

"Here it comes." My heart pounded in my chest. I hit Pause and sucked in a deep breath.

Rue gave me a quick grin then looked at the screen.

"Okay, let's see if we can get a look at the guy behind the wheel." I tapped the plus sign on the zoom bar, and the image on the screen increased in size. I frowned. "Not the best clarity. The guy is fuzzy. Is there a passenger with him?"

Rue squinted and leaned in. "Yeah, it looks like it, but that person is even fuzzier. Of course, no front plate either."

I looked for something on the front that could identify the vehicle then noticed the emblem on the grille. I pointed. "There. It's a Ford, and since there aren't any windows on the sides, it would be considered a panel van. That'll definitely help with the BOLO."

The van passed the first camera and continued on. Lee switched to the north camera, and since the vehicle following the van blocked the rear plate, we couldn't get a read on that either.

"Damn it." I was frustrated and thought we were going to lose the vehicle when it made a right turn into the alley. "What the hell? Where is he going?"

Lee spoke up. "The only thing back there is the post office docks and employee parking, the back of the gourmet popcorn store, and the employee parking spaces and entrance to Sparky's on the other corner."

My mind went back to what George had said earlier. I took a picture of the camera's time stamp, stood, and tipped my head at Rue. We needed to go. We thanked Lee for the help and left.

"Are you thinking what I'm thinking?" Rue asked after we walked out.

"Probably. What is T. J.'s actual name?"

"Hell if I know. Never had a reason to ask him."

"Come on. We need to talk to George again."

We returned to Sparky's a half hour after we'd left. I waved George down and told him it was urgent that we talk to him again. He led the way to his office with concern written across his face.

"What's up, guys?"

"George, did T. J. work last Monday afternoon?"

"Um, let me double-check. That was a while ago, and my memory isn't as good as it used to be."

We waited while he pulled up the employee schedule on the computer.

"Yep, he clocked in at six minutes before three. Why?"

"What is T. J.'s actual name?"

"Teddy Jennison."

"And he up and quit without any notice at all?"

"Yep, that's exactly what he did."

"And you've never seen him get in or out of a white van?"

"Nope, but T. J. works split shifts a lot. I wouldn't be out in the alley when he arrived or left."

"Have you ever seen a white van parked back there?" Rue asked.

"Not that I recall."

"Okay, we'll need his home address right away and his emergency contact's name, phone number, and their address."

"Sure thing." George pulled up T. J.'s personnel file and wrote everything down. "Here you go. Did T. J. do something wrong?"

"Not sure yet, George, but we appreciate your help."

Rue and I headed out. We were barely out the door, and I already had the phone pinned to my ear with Royce on the other end. I told him we had intel that could break the case. I said we needed to know everything he could find on a Teddy Jennison and that we would be back in five minutes to explain why.

Chapter 41

As soon as we got to the precinct, we stormed down the hallway and into Royce's office.

"So what the hell is going on? I looked up a Ted, Teddy, and Theodore Jennison and didn't find a damn thing to incriminate him. You sure you're barking up the right tree?"

"Here's what we know, Boss." I took a seat, and Rue mirrored my actions. "We found the white van and followed it to the alley behind Sparky's. That was last Monday at a few minutes before three in the afternoon."

Royce nodded for me to continue. "And?"

"And when we were there earlier to look at more footage, George, the manager said that T. J. up and quit, through a text message no less, saying that he and his brother were buying a boat and that he was taking time away from the day-to-day workforce."

"Sounds weird, but that doesn't make him a killer. He doesn't own a white van either. He has a 2016 silver Honda Fit."

"But his brother might. Plus, how does he intend to

support himself for an indefinite period of time without a job and still have money to buy a boat? Sounds like someone with money stashed."

"What's his brother's name, who is his family, and where do they live?"

"No clue yet, but we'll find that out soon enough. George gave me T. J.'s emergency contact names. I've also got his address so we can check his residence for a white van."

"We need a viable reason for a judge to issue a warrant, and quitting one's job isn't reason enough. We need more. Go grab a car out of impound, drive to his home, and see if that van is there. If it is, call me with the plate number so we can find out who it belongs to. We need probable cause, or we'll never get that warrant. Meanwhile, I'll follow up with that emergency contact."

After taking a picture of the paper George had written the information down on, I handed it to Royce.

Rue and I headed to the impound lot and chose a black 2017 Dodge Ram. I wanted something reliable enough to get us from point A to point B without breaking down.

Minutes later, I rolled past the house on record for Ted Jennison, saw a silver Honda Fit in the driveway, then continued on. At the end of the block, I turned around and parked along the curb two houses away.

"Shit. Sitting here isn't going to help us," Rue said. "That van could be in the garage for all we know."

I pointed through the windshield. "See that side door to the garage?"

"Yeah."

"See the window in said door?"

"I do."

"Good. Go peek through it and see if the van is

inside. I can't run if something goes sideways. Bum leg, you know."

Rue climbed out. He looked back in before closing the door. "How long are you going to drag out the healing-leg bullshit?"

I laughed. "As long as it serves me well. Plus, I'm the lead detective, and I have to stay healthy. Hey."

Rue looked back. "What?"

"Be careful."

He rolled his eyes and walked away.

Devon casually headed down the sidewalk. I knew he was checking his surroundings, although he did it well and without looking obvious. Once Rue reached the side yard, he darted to the edge of the house, crept along the wall to the garage door, and gave the window a quick side peek. After that, he pressed his hands along the sides of his face and looked in for a good ten seconds. Rue dashed back to the truck and climbed in.

"Well?"

He let out a hard breath. "Well, it's in there, but there's no chance of getting the plate number with the rear of the van by the overhead door."

"Did you turn the doorknob?"

"Are you serious?"

"No. We'd catch hell. I'll call Royce and see what he suggests."

I dialed our sergeant's desk phone, and Royce picked up. "See it?"

"Yeah, but it's in the garage. No chance of getting a plate number."

"Okay, stay put. I'm trying to get through to the parents in Hilton Head, but if the guys make a move, follow them."

I hung up and thought about the van. It was likely

that the brothers were worried about it being seen and that was why it was in the garage. I dialed Royce back. "Boss, we can't just sit back and do nothing, especially when we don't know if Gina is dead or alive. We need that warrant. She could be inside the house, and they could be torturing her for all we know. Don't we have enough probable cause? People confirmed a white van at the trooper sighting. The 911 call was about a female abduction in a light-colored van—likely Gina. T. J. was dropped off at work in a white van, and then just a day after Gina's abduction, he quits his bartending job. He said he wasn't going to work for a while and that he and his brother were going to buy a boat. That means they have enough cash to get along fine without jobs. They're going to disappear and keep doing what they're doing if we don't arrest them now. I bet that house holds plenty of incriminating evidence."

Royce groaned. "All good points. I'll call Judge Laughlin, plead our case, and get back to you as soon as I hear something."

We stared at the house for another hour, then I saw movement. I elbowed Rue, who was scrolling through his phone.

"Hey, they're up to something."

The overhead lifted, and the brothers walked out, each pulling a suitcase, along with duffel bags slung across their shoulders.

"Shit, they're going to make a run for it, and if they head across the river, we won't have jurisdiction anymore. I've got to tell Royce." I prayed he would answer on the first ring, and he did. "Boss, they're making a run for it. They're loading duffel bags and suit-cases in the trunk of the Honda Fit. If they cross the river, we're screwed."

"Damn it. I've got the judge on the other line. Hold on."

The phone went silent.

"Shit. I'm on hold!" I pounded the steering wheel as I waited.

Royce returned to the phone. "Okay, the judge says he'll have the warrant to me in ten minutes."

"They'll be gone by then, and we don't have it in our hands."

"Detain them, then. Go block their exit. I'll get Patrol to lend a hand."

I hung up, turned over the engine, and slammed the shifter into Drive. The tires squealed as the truck shot forward. The brothers had already gotten into the car and were backing up right when I reached the driveway. I couldn't see who was behind the wheel, but they gunned it and smashed into the nose of the truck.

"That's how you want to play this? That Honda is no match for this pickup." I gunned the truck and pushed the car up the driveway until it was jammed against the back of the van. The front end looked like an accordion. Both brothers leapt out and ran through yards as they tried to escape. I couldn't chase them, but Rue was in hot pursuit.

We weren't equipped with a police radio, and as I was about to dial 911, the patrol units rolled up. I yelled out that the brothers were on foot and running through yards to get away and that Rue was in pursuit. They took off after them. I called Royce and told him what was happening.

"I'm on my way with the warrant. I'll be there in five, and Forensics is right behind me."

I hung up, headed to the van, and luckily was able to read the plate number. I called it in and found out it was registered to a Chase Jennison of Macon, Georgia. Now all we needed was for Forensics to spray Luminol in the back of that van and the Jennison brothers' goose would be cooked.

Royce arrived within minutes, waving the document as he exited the cruiser. "Go for it!"

Between Rue and Patrol, they would locate the brothers and take them into custody quickly. The first thing I wanted to do was see what was in those duffel bags.

Royce and I gloved up, and I popped the hatch of the Honda.

"How much you want to bet these bags are literally full of blood money?"

Royce grimaced then jerked his head toward the bags. "Open them, and my bet says you're one hundred percent right."

I unzipped the duffel bags and peeked in. They were filled with banded cash. I would leave everything as we found it so Forensics could take pictures and run tests. Royce looked over his shoulder at Martin and Billy as they walked up the driveway.

"Photograph everything and spray the back of that van. We need to see if Gina is in the house."

I knew Royce was kidding himself. T. J. and Chase wouldn't leave if there was still a living, breathing person in their home. That would be throwing away money in their eyes.

We walked the house and found nobody dead or alive inside. Forensics would take their pictures, then we would spend more time inside gathering information.

I opened the van's sliding door and let out a whistle. "Have a look at this, Boss."

Royce looked inside, saw the ropes and eye bolts,

then dropped his head and cursed. "I can't even imagine—"

"Me neither."

I turned as I heard cars pull up behind us. The patrol units were back, and they'd captured both brothers.

Rue climbed out of one of the cars, looking sweaty and disheveled. He grinned anyway. "It took a little coaxing with our sidearms, but we got 'em, Boss."

"Nice work, boys. Read those pieces of shit their rights, take them to the station, and we'll deal with them later."

I walked to the patrol car T. J. was sitting in and pulled open the door. "Guess you'll have to wait on that boat, buddy. Doesn't look like the life of leisure is in the cards for you after all." I slammed the door and returned to Rue and Royce's side.

Chapter 42

It was already late in the day, well past shift change. Royce went over everything at our meeting with Bleu and the night shift team. They would go through Teddy's home, search it inch by inch, and catalog everything related to the abductions and murders of Valerie, LeAnn, and the trooper. Gina was still questionable since we hadn't recovered her remains, but in my gut, I knew she was dead. If there were more people that we didn't know about, I would do my best to get that information when Rue and I conducted the interrogation tomorrow.

Since we were familiar with T. J., Royce promised that we could conduct the interview and find out what had prompted him and his brother to commit such heinous crimes. I assumed it was the lure of money and the carnal pleasures that cash would give two very average brothers.

I planned to ask more about their formative years tomorrow, but what Royce gathered from his call to the parents was that they hadn't spent much time with Chase and Teddy when the boys needed them most.

That night, I would go home, give thanks that nobody else would die at the hands of Ted and Chase Jennison, and appreciate my family and loved ones.

I gave Rue a shoulder pat as we walked to our cars. "Hey, pal, why not come to my house for supper? We have a lot to be thankful for, and my family is your family. It wouldn't be right if you celebrated alone."

Devon grinned. "You sure?"

"Absolutely."

"Okay, that sounds pretty nice. I'll be right behind you."

At home, we enjoyed a great dinner with my family and said only that our latest bad guys had been captured and were behind bars. Young kids like Chloe and Della didn't need to hear the details. They were smitten with Rue anyway, and just having him there for supper was enough to keep them smiling.

After we ate, Devon and I sat outside on the deck and discussed tomorrow's interrogation. We needed to ask the brothers who their buyers were, and even if they wouldn't reveal the names, we hoped the state police would find those individuals and take them into custody.

I wanted to know why they killed. What led them to commit such hideous crimes against other human beings? I wondered if certain people were predisposed to be killers or if there was a trigger. Was one the leader and the other the follower, and what role, or lack of one, did their parents play in the brothers' upbringing? I didn't have those answers, but I was sure they did. Maybe they'd talk, and maybe they'd lawyer up. And last, would they tell us what they had done with Gina's body so her family could lay her to rest?

Tomorrow would be filled with tough questions and even tougher-to-hear answers, but we needed to know everything. We would pit one brother against the other and lie to their faces to get those answers before they clammed up and demanded lawyers. The families of the victims deserved to know why their loved ones had been chosen and whether they'd suffered before dying.

It was almost ten o'clock by the time Rue rose to leave. The kids had gone to bed an hour earlier, and Mom and Marie sat at the dining room table while playing Scrabble.

"I'm heading out," Rue said, "and thanks so much for a great supper. Good night."

I walked out with Devon and said I'd see him in the morning.

"Have a stiff drink or two, Cannon. I know you aren't one to fall asleep easily."

I knuckled the car's doorframe. "Good idea. Drive safe, partner." I watched as Rue drove away until I couldn't see his taillights any longer.

Chapter 43

At the morning briefing, the night crew said they'd found knives, duct tape, and zip ties in a tote in a bedroom closet.

Forensics passed on that the van lit up like a Christmas tree after Luminol was sprayed in the rear area. They had gathered blood and hair samples that would be tested against the remains of the bodies we'd found.

Royce had gotten word that the state police were making headway. They'd heard through reliable sources that an underground group of people might be working out of Augusta in the organ-trafficking trade. Their officers would work hand in hand with the FBI on that side of the investigation.

I couldn't wait to sit across from Ted—or T. J. as we'd known him over the years. I'd never had any inkling that he was capable of cold-blooded murder for profit and wondered if everything began after Chase came to town. According to their profiles, Chase was older by two years, and if it was true that the parents hadn't done much child rearing, Chase could very well be the leader, the parent figure, and the one who'd called the shots from childhood on. I hoped to find out everything as soon as our meeting wrapped up.

It was after eight thirty by the time the meeting adjourned. Rue and I headed to our jail wing and asked the guard to put each brother in a separate room. Our intentions were to interview Ted first. He was sure to be uncomfortable talking to us, and maybe that would work in our favor. If he was indeed the follower rather than the leader, it could be easier to persuade him to talk, especially if we told a few white lies to get him going.

After we were given the go-ahead, Rue and I watched T. J. through the one-way glass before entering the interrogation room. He appeared jittery, and that was good. Sitting alone in a cell all night without Chase telling him what to say and how to act had likely given Ted plenty of time to think about his actions and the consequences. He had to know he would likely spend life in prison, and I was sure that scared the shit out of him. We would be his friends, his allies, but only if he leveled with us. Chase couldn't help him anymore.

He glanced up when we entered the room. What looked like a mix of anger and disappointment was written across his face. I wondered if the disappointment was only because they had been caught and not because of remorse. Their dreams of living the high life had evaporated into thin air. He returned his attention to his folded hands and kept quiet. Rue and I took seats across from him and stared until he finally looked at us.

"So, Teddy, or would you rather be called T. J.? I mean, that's the guy we've known for two years. The friendly bartender who didn't look like he had an evil bone in his body."

He remained silent.

I continued. "We'll call you T. J., then. Anyway, it looks like you're up shit creek. Chase ratted you out, said you had a dream about a great way of making money and invited him to come to Savannah so you could carry out that fantasy. Something about you being sick and tired of living such an ordinary life. Something about your parents? What was that about?"

"That bastard. It was his idea, every bit of it. It's all lies except the part about our parents. They were ordinary people—actually lowlife losers—who got lucky. My old man won big at the casino, their home away from home. We were in our early teens and rebellious like most kids that age, and our folks quickly realized that we hindered their new lifestyle. They cleaned up well when money was involved, but Chase and I were still an embarrassment. Mom and Dad began associating with rich people who didn't have two punk sons who lacked ambition. Those people had kids in boarding schools in other countries. Chase and I were home alone most of the time and raised ourselves. We caused even more trouble as we got older, but then Chase moved to Macon for a girlfriend."

"That had to be tough, but then Chase came back into the picture. He wanted that rich lifestyle, too, and told you about his new idea, right?"

T. J. nodded. "Chase was the leader our whole lives. He left Macon, returned to Savannah, and told me the plan. We could be rich, just like our parents were. I was afraid, but he said to think of it as hunting. We've killed animals before and gutted them right in the field. Once the money started coming in and was in front of me, I couldn't take my eyes off of it. I was committed. It was like a drug, and we were going to buy a huge boat and live the life of leisure."

"There's always consequences, but deep down, I'm thinking you wanted your parents' approval."

He ignored my comment. "Are we going to prison?"

Rue chuckled. "What do you think? You've murdered at least three people that we know of and sold their organs for profit. Are there more?"

"Not that I was involved in."

I gave Rue a concerned glance. "Meaning?"

"Like I said, it was all Chase's idea. I don't know what he did before he came back home. You'll have to ask him."

"You don't sound remorseful."

He shrugged. "Too late for that now. What's done is done. What about all the money we earned? I'll need a good lawyer."

I pulled back. "Wow." I was dumbstruck and could barely think of what to say.

Rue took over. "You didn't earn it. You murdered for it, and life doesn't work that way, kid. You'll get a public defender and likely never see the light of day again. Hopefully, that money will go to the families of the people you and your sick brother slaughtered. They have loved ones to bury."

I looked at Rue. "I don't know about you, but I'm done here. I feel the need to wash up."

"One more question before we go," Rue said. "Where are Gina's remains?"

"We tossed them in a dumpster in Augusta, but I don't remember where."

Rue shook his head. "And who are the buyers?"

Teddy smiled. "That was two questions. I'm done talking without a deal."

"Nope," I said. "There aren't any deals on the table. Karma is a bitch, T. J."

He rattled his fingers on the table. "I'm not following."

"Chances are good that you and your brother will get shivved in prison. At least, I hope so. Maybe you won't die, and maybe you will. Either way, you'll feel the same pain those innocent people felt when you stuck your blade into them."

Rue and I stood and walked out. We didn't look back, and I didn't want to waste another minute of my life by talking to Chase. There was no way he was remorseful. Hell, T. J. wasn't, and his mind was still on the money. Lawrence and Bentley could take over. I was done.

Chapter 44

Two weeks later

Our shift was almost over, and as I gathered my things to leave, Royce rushed into our office. I hoped whatever he was going to say wouldn't delay me from heading where I was about to go.

I raised a brow. "What's up, Boss?"

"Just got a call from the state police. Ken Jarrett said they busted the organ-trafficking ring wide open, at least the one in Augusta that was related to the Jennison case."

"That's awesome news. I hope every last one of them rots in prison or worse."

Royce slapped the doorframe. "That calls for a celebratory drink. On me, of course."

"I'm up for that," Rue said.

"Yeah, I'll have to pass."

They both jerked their heads my way.

I raised my hands. "Okay, okay. I was going to surprise you in the morning. My new Vette is in, and I'm going to go pick it up. I was hoping you'd go with me, Rue."

Devon laughed. "Yeah, I'm not so sure I'm ready for that. Don't forget your track record. You crashed your beloved white Vette, then you destroyed the front end of that Ram when you slammed into T. J.'s car and pushed it up the driveway and into the van. You turned that car into a sardine can."

Royce chuckled as Rue carried on.

"My feelings are hurt, guys. I'm a great driver, and neither of those incidents were because I was at fault. It's the price one pays for being a damn good detective."

"How about this?" Royce said. "You go pick up the Vette, meet us at King's Bar and Grill, and then you can take us for a drive around the parking lot."

"Yeah, okay, but once you see her, I know you'll reconsider."

Lawrence and Bentley walked by. "What's going on? Reconsider what?"

Royce continued. "I'm buying drinks at King's Bar and Grill. Mitch is going to pick up his new Vette, then he'll come by and show it off to us. I said I'd take a ride around the parking lot with him."

"Can't wait to see it," Bentley said. "You've been waiting a long time for that beauty. Congrats, Mitch."

"Thanks, buddy."

Rue grinned. "Okay, Cannon. The hell with it. I'll be happy to go pick it up with you, and you can even let her rip. After all, what are partners for?"

I laughed as I headed out the door. "Now you're talking my language."

THE END

Thank you!

Thanks for reading *Fear for Your Life*, Book Five in the Detective Mitch Cannon Savannah Heat Thriller Series. I hope you enjoyed it!

Find all my books leading up to this series at http://cmsutter.com

Stay abreast of my new releases by signing up for my VIP email list at: http://cmsutter.com/newsletter/

You'll be one of the first to get a glimpse of the cover reveals and release dates, and you'll have a chance at exciting raffles offered with each new release.

Posting a review will help other readers find my books. I appreciate every review, whether positive or negative, and if you have a second to spare, a review is truly appreciated.

Find me on Facebook at https://www.facebook.com/cmsutterauthor/